Seduc

Cyborg Seduction - Book Ten

By Laurann Dohner

Seducing Stag

by Laurann Dohner

Stag and the crew of the Varnish are on a mission, responding to a distress signal of a freighter that has been attacked by the Markus Models. Instead of finding the enemy, they discover one sole survivor. Nala's a human, and having suffered at their hands during his time on Earth, there's no species Stag despises more. But when the petite woman confuses him for an android and tries to order him around, Stag decides she'll live — and pay for her slights.

Nala Vestria has lost her freighter, her crew and her father, only to become personal maid to a cyborg. Stag is surly, short-tempered, and completely untrusting of humans…not to mention intense, commanding, and maybe the hottest being Nala has ever seen. When she finds him temporarily at her mercy, Nala isn't sure if she wants to kill him or kiss him. Then again, life is short. She opts for the latter.

Nala swiftly becomes a distraction Stag can't afford, especially after he's had a carnal taste of what the woman has to offer. He'll take her back to Garden, his home planet, and be rid of her — as well as the emotions she evokes. But as their journey home becomes harrowing, Nala may prove to be more of an asset than a liability. To both the ship…and the lonely cyborg who commands her.

Cyborg Seduction Series

Seducing Stag

Copyright © September 2016

Editor: Kelli Collins

Cover Art: Dar Albert

ISBN: 978-1-944526-66-5

Chapter One

"Spread out," Stag ordered the group of six men who followed him inside the damaged ship. "Someone silence that alarm." The blaring irritated him.

Kelis ripped open one of the access panels. The silence was welcome when he disconnected the right wires. Smoke lingered in the corridors but the fire-suppression system had worked. White foam stained the floors and walls. Stag took the lead position and gripped his weapon. Only one life sign registered and it came from the living quarters.

He glanced around a curve and stared at the severely damaged android sprawled on the floor a few feet away. It had been torn to pieces. The head was even smashed and ripped open. One of the arms on the disconnected body twitched. He saw no weapon marks.

"The Markus Models don't seem to like androids that aren't of their own models." He glanced at Veller.

The male shook his head. "Long-range sensors read the shuttle hasn't turned around. They are still headed away. I'll notify you if they return so we have time to evacuate."

"They could have left some of their units aboard and they might not register as life signs. Don't let your guard down," Stag warned. He rounded the corner and stepped over the mutilated body of the android. It clearly wasn't a threat. He kept his weapon trained forward and stopped at the first door. He waited while Kelis overrode the lock. The door opened to a small crew quarter.

Stag clenched his teeth, disgusted at the sight of that much blood and what was left of the Earther. He'd been torn apart as well, portions of his corpse strewn about the space. The biggest pieces of him intact were the head and chest. Blood stains marked almost every inch of wall, floor, and ceiling. He guessed it had happened within hours.

Kelis peered in. "Overkill."

"Understatement," Stag muttered. "I'm tempted to leave now. We've seen enough."

"There is still one life sign aboard," Veller reminded him. "We might be able to get valuable information from the Earther, like how many Markus Models were here. The computer banks have been fried. Maze is in the command center and he said there's nothing to retrieve. Every system except life support has been purposely damaged."

Stag moved to the next door to find it wasn't locked. Two bodies lay inside. They were intact but bloodied. One lay on the floor with an obvious broken neck and battered features. The other one, dumped into a chair, had suffered torture. His contorted limbs showed severe trauma. Neither had survived their attacks.

"What were the Markus Models doing? Practicing how to kill by various methods?"

Stag held Kelis's gaze. "Perhaps."

"Sick bastards."

Stag silently agreed. They checked two more rooms, finding one more body. It had been stripped bare and dissected. Bile rose but Stag managed to stifle the urge to lose his last meal on the floor. The Markus Models had pinned the male Earther to the floor by jamming metal into his limbs and sliced him open as if they'd wanted to see his insides. Various organs lay on the floor next to him, and the blood patterns suggested he'd still been alive when they'd started.

"Fuck," Kelis snarled, turning away. "I'm glad you ordered Maze to go to Control instead of with us, as he wanted to."

Stag backed out of the room and the door closed. "As a medic, he'd want to rescue the crew, and I doubted he'd be able to do anything for them. He agonizes over death. We know the Markus Models have no regard for life. I think your assessment was correct. They were running experiments on these Earthers."

"Let's go. I don't want to see what's left of the one with a heartbeat. He probably won't be able to talk." Kelis shook his head. "This was more than enough."

"It's possible he hid." Yammer stepped forward. "Otherwise he'd be dead too."

"Unlikely," Veller disagreed. "Markus Models can read life signs as well as we can. They would have tracked it the way we are. There's still an active sign in the captain's quarters."

"It might be a Markus Model." Kelis removed his secondary weapon. "I say we kill the murdering freak, right after we get information from it."

8

"Agreed." Stag took the lead again. "They don't go down easy. Try to damage the body but avoid head shots. We can remove its memory core and hack into it."

"No frying the bastard then," Kelis muttered. "Great."

They reached the last door and found it locked. Stag nodded at Veller, and he came forward to tear off the panel and override the mechanism. Stag tensed, using a hand signal to give his men orders before the door opened.

The metal parted and they rushed inside. The living quarter consisted of one large room and an open cleansing unit. The sight that greeted them left Stag stunned.

An older Earther male lay face down in a pool of blood, but it was the bed that captured his attention. It was a massive four-poster—and a pale, nude body had been strung upright against the headboard.

It was a female. Her arms and legs were spread wide apart, bound upright to the tall bed posts at the head of the bed. Her head was dipped, long blonde hair falling down her body to her waist. The mass of curls mostly covered her bared breasts. Some blood stained her creamy white skin, stark in comparison. There were smears of it near her wrists, ankles, and waist. One perfectly displayed bloody handprint showed on her inner thigh, as if someone had gripped her there.

Stag kept his weapon trained on her as he approached. He took note of her chest rising and falling, although it was slight. He glanced lower. The small patch of pubic hair matched the rest of her. She wasn't a big female, but fully grown if her breast size and body were any indication.

9

One of his men muttered something but he didn't catch the words. The female didn't respond or make any movement.

"It could be a trap. Check the room for explosive devices. She looks like bait." Stag froze while he waited.

"She's alive." Kelis came forward. "I'll get her down."

Stag knocked him back. "Did you hear me? Check the bed for devices. There's no way to reach her without walking on it."

His men went to work and Stag studied the woman. She *was* breathing. Her breasts moved just slightly. He took in the ties that held her. She'd been bound tightly, stretched as if she were a living canvas.

"Shit," Parqel rasped. "Good call." He got to his feet by the head of the bed. "It's pressure rigged on all four feet of the bed. Any weight change and I assume it will blow up. I see wires leading into the mattress, hidden by the covers on first glance."

Kelis moved to stand next to him. "How did you know?"

Stag hesitated. "Most men would have rushed toward a sexually appealing woman. It makes sense to me why they'd leave *her* alive, but none of the men onboard this ship."

Veller spoke. "We could kill gravity and float to cut her down."

Stag shook his head. "Remove gravity and the bed would shift as well, releasing the triggers."

"How are we going to get her down?" Kelis sounded frustrated.

"We aren't." Stag turned to his men. "Let's go."

"We can't just leave her," Kelis argued. "She's alive. We can try to disarm the device."

"Tell him what would happen, Parqel," Stag demanded.

The other cyborg sighed. "I cut the wires and it will go off. I can't reach the device without putting weight on the bed. We can't even cut her from the sides and lift her down because her weight is part of the bed."

"She was dead the moment they made her a trap." Stag stared at the woman. He felt pity. "We'll cut life support so there are no life signs to draw others to the freighter. It will be a painless way for her to go."

"It's a *woman*." Kelis faced him. "We can't just leave her to die."

"I find this distasteful as well. But there's no way to save her without that explosion killing us too."

"I'll stay behind and wait for you to leave this ship, then attempt it. That way only my life will be at risk."

"I won't allow you to die for a human, Kelis."

"Damn it!" the cyborg shouted. "I must try, Stag."

A soft sound came from the bed and Stag turned his head. The woman lifted her chin, her hair moving to reveal her generous breasts, just enough to show one perky nipple. He studied her. She had delicate, attractive features and pale blue eyes.

She seemed a bit disorientated as she blinked, focusing on him. Confusion was an easy emotion to read, but then a hint of fear showed.

She glanced away from him, noticing his men. He stepped to the end of the bed, watching her.

She looked down, closed her eyes, and then opened them. "Who is in charge?" She had a soft, pleasant voice.

"I am."

She peered directly at Stag, then to the weapon in his hand, then back to hold his gaze. "You're cyborgs, aren't you?"

"Yes."

"I figured. I've only heard of one thing that has gray skin." She licked her lips. "There's an explosive device in the bed. You can't reach me without it going off. I calculate there's enough there to take out this entire section and probably blow a hole in the outer hull. Did any of my crew survive?"

"*Your* crew?"

"I'm the captain." She seemed to notice the body on the floor and tears filled her eyes. "That's my father. He's dead, isn't he?"

Stag saw no reason to lie. "Yes."

"What were those things that boarded us? Do you know?"

"Markus Models. They are flesh-exterior androids. Do you know how many there were?"

"I saw three. I could hear someone screaming though. I think it was Melvin. He's a few rooms down. I'll assume he had a reason to scream. That means at least four. They looked like identical clones but they were really strong. I shot one of them twice in the chest but he just kept

12

coming. He hit me and it was lights out until I woke while they were tearing off my clothes. I thought they were going to rape me but they strung me up instead and cut open the mattress to plant a bomb. Then they made the bed." She glanced at the corpse on the floor. "He wasn't in here then. One of them struck me again and I passed out...until now."

"Your entire crew is dead. You were the only life sign."

The pain of grief twisted up her features but she masked it fast, seeming to pull her emotions together. "Thank you for answering our distress signal and trying to come to our aid." She opened her hands and gripped the bonds. "Can you do me a favor? Please set the auto-destruct sequence on my ship before you leave. They're planning on coming back. We're hauling sex bots in cargo two. The crates state it's mining equipment but that's what the real cargo is. They figured that out somehow. They were talking aloud when they were putting me up here. They think they can reprogram those bots to be useful to them. Blow me all to hell. I don't want them to get a damn thing. I also don't want to be alive when they return."

She paused. "You can take the bots if you want but don't let those bastards have them. Hurry, whatever you decide to do. They were out of range of communicating with someone and needed to leave the ship. I don't think they were willing to use satellite relay. That means ship-to-ship coms only, and you know the range on those isn't that great. My ship was too slow to make some rendezvous point they'd set up. I don't know how long they've been gone."

"Why aren't you asking us to save you?" Stag was intrigued by her, curious.

"It's suicide. I'm sure you have better things to do today than die. So did I, but I'm the one who got boarded. They didn't register on our long-range sensors. Hell, we didn't even know we'd been boarded until they were already inside and attacking us."

"They probably hacked your computer system and overrode your sensors." Veller frowned. "We figure they left about an hour ago."

"Do you know who they went to meet?" Stag drew her attention by stepping closer.

"Brothers. That's all I know. No clue who they are or what that means."

"More Markus Models." Kelis sighed. "They will probably return with at least one more shuttle. They destroyed your freighter. It's not traveling anywhere. They wanted it dead in space. This ship has a large cargo capacity but it's too slow for them. They'll probably have to divide the cargo."

"Check the cargo bay and make certain they didn't leave any models behind to guard the bots." Stag glanced at Kelis. "Transfer what you can onto our ship, destroy the rest." He regarded Veller. "You heard her. See if you can set the auto destruct. If not, we'll blow it when we leave. Go. Stick together in teams."

His men left and Stag stared at the woman. "You're very brave."

"That's not the word I'd go with." She glanced down her body. "I look like I belong in one of those bondage clubs located on Mars. I would have shaved my legs this morning if I'd known."

Stag examined her body.

"Eyes up here, gorgeous," she murmured. "You don't need to verify that. It was a bad joke."

He held her gaze.

"I guess I should be thankful you're not human. Most men would have come at me looking like this and set off the bombs." She smiled. "Those Markus models would have been able to steal my cargo, since it's on the other side of the ship sealed in the hold, and still gotten me killed. That would have pissed me off."

"Why did you call me that?"

"Gorgeous? Because you are. You've got beautiful black hair and those blue eyes. It gets lonely in space. My father always hired the crew, and not one of them was much to look at or sexually appealing. He did that on purpose." She tried to wiggle her body a little but the bonds held her too tight. "God, this is unpleasant. It feels like I've been turned into a wishbone."

"Stop fighting and loosen your muscles. It will hurt less."

"Been strung up much?"

"A few times in the past," he admitted.

"Why would someone do that to you? All they'd have to do is shut you down if they wanted you in one place."

She believed he was an android. He wasn't surprised by her assumption. "I have no shutoff function. It was punishment. They whipped us."

"Why would anyone pay that kind of money and then damage something like you?" She shook her head. "A guy must have owned you, and his wife probably wished you were upgraded with the right equipment to be in her bedroom. Did he take it out on you? You're really handsome." She ran her gaze over his body. "Nice measurement designs too. My father said some of you were used for sex bots way back when. I can see why. Hell, I'd buy you if I'd ever seen you in one of the sex-bot ads."

His temper flared. "You'd buy me to have sex with you?"

"I'm trying to distract myself from the pain." She rolled her head, looking away from him, and fought the restraints. "Please blow the ship. This is agony."

"I'm not an android."

She stopped moving, staring at him. "You're a cyborg. Sorry. Do you differentiate yourself from them? I heard you were programmed with some mimicked emotions. I didn't mean to insult you. Don't get your circuits overloaded. I'm just having a shit day and I'm ready for it to be over. My father is dead and so is my crew. It's also irritating that something that looks like *you* is standing in my bedroom under these dire circumstances. Talk about irony."

"Explain."

"I'm naked and restrained, you're like sex on legs, though you don't have the right equipment or the programming to touch me. Plus, the whole big *boom* if you climb on the bed to reach me. See where this is heading? I'm fucked but not in the fun way."

His temper flared more. She'd buy him to have sex with her and she didn't believe he was a sentient being. It proved his point that all Earthers were the same. He watched her struggle in the restraints, her hair shifting to reveal her nipples. She did have a beautiful body. The blood marring her skin didn't appear to be hers.

"Do you need orders to go?" She looked at him. "Go. Take the cargo if you can use it somehow. You can't save me, if you have some program that tells you to try. Disregard it. Get off the ship and blow it to hell."

He suddenly didn't want her to die. He wanted to keep her alive. He stared at the bed. "How did they rig the bomb?"

"What?"

"How did they rig it? You said you saw them do it."

"They pulled the covers off the top and cut into the mattress. It's too complicated for you. You're an old model. Just go. That's an order."

He approached the bed and pulled back the covers, making certain they remained on top of the mattress. He saw where they'd opened the mattress, the device exposed to his view.

"Listen," she demanded. "Back away from the bed. You're going to blow us both up and those dickhead skin android things are going to get the cargo. Fuck that. They killed me and my crew. I'm already toast. Get off the ship and blow it!"

He leaned forward, studying the device. It was complicated. He removed his com and contacted Veller. "Return to the captain's quarters now."

"Hey, gorgeous face?"

He looked up at her, infuriated. "My name is Stag."

"Abort your rescue mission. It's doomed to fail. Do you understand? I'm giving you a direct order. I know they discontinued your models because there was some kind of problem with you guys taking orders, but you have to be smart. You escaped Earth before they shut all your models down. Leave this ship before the bed blows. Do you understand?"

He glared at her.

She glared back. "Abort. Stop. What word triggers you to do what you're told?"

"Say 'please'."

That response seemed to surprise her but she recovered fast. "Please take orders. Get off this ship and blow it up."

He gave her a cold stare. "I'm not a robot or an android."

"I don't care what the hell you are. You want reasoning and logic? I know *my* androids appreciate that. There's no way to get me off these posts without blowing a big hole into the side of the ship. It will decompress this entire section and suck everything into space. Those fucked-up flesh bot things will return and take my cargo. They win! I don't want that. I want them to return to find out they did all this for nothing! Do you *get* that?"

"I do. I fully plan to make certain they return to nothing."

"Good. Go."

Veller entered the room. "What is it?"

He stepped out of the way. "Look at this. Can you disarm it?"

Veller came forward, bent, careful not to touch the bed. "I know this."

"Good. Can you disarm it?"

"No, but Hellion can."

"Are you certain?"

"It's fully contained. There's no way to open the casing without triggering it to explode. I should have thought of this. It requires a signal hack to shut it down. It's the perfect device for a Markus Model to use."

Stag connected with his ship. "Send Hellion now."

It took a few minutes. The burly cyborg entered and came to a dead stop, openly gawking at the woman. "Dreams really do come true. I am definitely up for this mission."

"Shut up," Stag snapped, imagining where the male's thoughts had gone. "The bed is rigged with an explosive device."

"It's a reguletta 643AB9," Veller informed him. "You have much better hacking skills than I do with devices like these. Can you shut it off?"

Hellion kept staring at the woman.

"Do it," Stag growled. "Stop staring at her."

"I'm working and appreciating the view," Hellion muttered. "I can multitask." A slight hum sounded. Hellion grinned. "It's off. Can I cut her down?"

Stag holstered his weapon and grabbed the blade strapped to his outer thigh. He gripped the post and lifted his leg, stepping up onto the bed. He got right in front of the woman, looking down at her. "What's your name?"

"Captain Nala Vestria."

He bent, slashing at the binds at her ankles. Her legs immediately dropped together. He straightened, freed her arms, then threw her over his shoulder. She didn't weigh much. He turned, holding her in place as he jumped off the bed. She gasped.

He snagged the bedding off the mattress and tossed it over the top of her. Veller and Hellion stared at him.

Stag pointed to the door. "Finish transferring what cargo you can onto our ship. I've got her."

"I'd be more than happy to carry her." Hellion held out his arms. "I know you don't like Earthers."

"Put me down!" the woman demanded. She wiggled against his shoulder. "I can walk."

He reached up and placed a hand on her lower back, pinning her to his shoulder, hooking his other arm tighter around her legs. The blanket covered her lower body. "You weren't here when she said she'd *buy me* if I'd been in an ad for sex bots."

Hellion's arms dropped and his mouth parted, shock slackening his features. Veller arched both eyebrows but masked his reaction otherwise.

"I saved her life, so she owes me. My price is, she's going to know what it feels like to be treated like an android. I won't harm her—but I *will* teach her a lesson. Follow my orders." He strode forward, carrying the woman out of the room.

"I technically saved her," Hellion called out. "*I* want to be her sex bot."

"Over my dead body." Stag kept going.

Chapter Two

Nala struggled but the big bastard was strong and fast. It didn't help that her skin was slick from the cleansing unit he'd shoved her into. He blocked her route to the door, grabbed the clothes he'd slung over his shoulder and offered them to her.

She identified each piece. He must have ordered one of his men to collect some of her things from her ship. She took the pants and shirt, quickly putting them on.

"You're confined to quarters. I've blocked your ability to control anything inside the room." He crossed his arms over his chest and backed away. "You'll find clean bedding in the storage drawer in the wall, next to the end of the bunk. I expect the sheets to be changed when I get back, and for you to have also picked up the room." He pointed out the laundry chute, the panel where he kept some cleaning supplies stored, and then smiled. "I'll think up other tasks for you later today. Right now, I have things to do."

She just gaped at him, stunned.

"I always wanted a cleaning android. Now I have one."

"Have you gone crazy?"

"I'm *angry*. I'm tired of you Earthers thinking cyborgs are animated robots with gray flesh. I'm as sentient as you are. It's irritating to be treated otherwise. You'll learn. Get to work, droid."

"I won't."

"You have to earn your food. That should motivate you to do as you're told." He spun, touched the panel by the door, and it opened. He left fast, the door sealing her inside.

Nala stood there, reeling. He meant it.

She glanced around his quarters. They were already clean. Some of her crew were messy, but Stag definitely wasn't. "Son of a bitch."

The door opened and she spun, expecting him to have returned, maybe tell her he'd been joking.

A new cyborg came in, carrying a medical scanner and a case.

"I'm a medic. Take a seat, Nala."

She moved to the only place to sit and rested her behind on the edge of the bed. The cyborg turned on his scanner, running it over her head, then lower.

"Do you have a name or number to call you?"

"Maze. Are you experiencing any pain? Headache? Ringing in your ears? Metallic taste in your mouth?"

"I have a little bit of a headache but I was knocked out twice."

"That's what I heard. They seemed to have managed not to bruise your face with the strikes but I see a little redness." He crouched, running the scanner over her arms, then her middle section, and down both of her legs. He twisted, set down the scanner, and opened the case to withdraw a small box.

She immediately tensed when he withdrew an injector and tapped the control pad on the end of it. "What are you going to do?"

"You have no internal bleeding, no fractures, no concussion or broken bones. I also checked for any implants the Markus Models might have tagged you with." He looked at her then. "They didn't chip you for tracking."

That was a horrible thought she hadn't considered. "Good."

"I'm giving you a mild dosage for pain to alleviate the headache and I'm taking a blood sample to run. I can get a better scope of your medical history that way. Have you been fully inoculated for space travel?"

"Yes."

"Excellent. Wrist, please."

She lifted one, exposing the bruising there.

He paused, touched the control pad, and sighed.

"What?"

"I didn't notice the bruising. It's severe. I've adjusted the medication I'm giving you to include something that will help you heal faster."

He pressed the injector against her skin and she winced a little when it went off. It didn't hurt but she felt a slight tap. The blood draw would leave a pin prick but very tiny. He returned the injector to the case, put it back inside the bag, and rose. "Have a good day."

She jumped up before he left. "Wait!"

He hesitated and peered back at her. "I'm not supposed to talk to you outside of medical issues."

"Why?"

"You're Stag's prisoner. You angered him."

24

"What about my rights? I demand to talk to an authority."

The cyborg faced her. "Stag is the authority on this vessel. He's in charge."

"My freighter was attacked, so how does that make me some kind of criminal? Are you saying I'm under arrest? For what? I'm registered."

"Stag has taken possession of you."

"I'm a *person*."

"You're an android. You have no rights."

Her mouth fell open again. "You just ran a scan on me. You know I'm one hundred percent human."

"I'm aware, but those are his orders. You're to be treated as an android."

"This is crazy."

"Agreed."

"So you know it's wrong. *Do* something. Please."

He gave her a pity look. "He won't harm you. He gave the crew his word, and he would never lie."

"He is if he's saying I'm an android!"

"He wants to teach you a lesson, and to be frank, Stag isn't one you want to anger. He has a temper. No one on this crew will go against his orders unless they feel he's crossed a line into cruelty. He wouldn't do that. I strongly suggest you apologize to him after he has time to reevaluate this situation." He spun around and tapped the panel. The door opened and he was gone before she could stop him again.

25

"Damn it!" She wanted to stomp her foot. Were all cyborgs crazy? They must be. She crossed the room and tried to open the door but it wouldn't respond.

She returned to the bed and sat down, then twisted and stretched out.

It had been a horrible day. Tears filled her eyes. She'd lost her crew, her ship, and her father. Now she was the prisoner of a malfunctioning cyborg. There were a lot of them, and they all seemed unaware of how many laws they were breaking by keeping her locked up. It wasn't a mystery anymore why Earth had decommissioned their models, if her interaction with them so far had been any example of their behavior. They flat-out refused to take orders or be logical.

Grief set in and she cried for all she'd lost. She'd worry about her future later.

* * * * *

Stag glanced at the small monitor in front of him and grimaced. The Earther was curled into a ball on his bed, sobbing. Guilt surfaced. He'd forgotten in his anger that her father had died, and she had to have cared about her murdered crew. It was tempting to return to his quarters to talk to her but the Markus Models were close. Priorities were clear.

He turned off the security feed and addressed his crew.

"Prepare to detonate that ship."

Hellion nodded. "Ready."

The coms beeped and Stag reached out, turning them on. "Report."

"I've checked over every crate transferred over. They haven't been tampered with. The Markus Models either didn't have time to attempt to reprogram them or were waiting until they picked them up later to do it. Not all of them would fit inside our hold. It's probably why the Markus Models couldn't transfer them into their shuttle."

"How many units were left behind?"

"Twelve, and I removed their theft-tracking systems. We managed to store eight. I rigged the remaining crates with small explosives and am awaiting your order to detonate. They will be damaged too severely to be salvaged and the blasts will be contained inside the cargo hold."

He trusted Veller's competence. He would have made certain the remaining bots couldn't be useful to the Markus Models. "Do that now. We're clear. Thank you." He cut coms.

"What are we going to do with the bots we brought aboard?" Kelis glanced at him.

Stag considered it. "Take them back home. I'm sure we'll find a use for them."

Hellion turned in his seat and grinned.

Stag shook his head. "I can't see the council opening up a brothel on Garden. I was thinking they could be reprogrammed for agricultural use."

Parqel chuckled. "Like Rune. Maybe she can teach the other sex bots to water plants naked as well. I know *I've* visited that section just for the view."

Hellion grunted. "Great." He swiveled his seat back. "Not all of us are in family units and have access to females."

27

Stag made a mental note to plan a trip to a sector with a brothel soon for his single men. He didn't voice that though. "Detonate the ship."

They watched on the main viewer as the transport self-destructed on command. It decompressed in sections, lights flashing, then began to break apart.

"Move us out of the debris field, then deploy our trackers and get us out of here. We can't fight off two shuttles. It would be pointless to try."

Hellion touched his console, doing as he'd been ordered. Minutes passed. "Five trackers launched." He paused. "I hope they work."

"I do too. They are out of the debris path, correct?"

"Yes."

"Good. We put a lot of time and effort into shielding them. They should attach to any ship that comes within range, once activated. With luck, we'll tag one of the models' ships. Let's go. Hellion, monitor us and turn them on once we're at a safe distance."

"You really think the Markus Models will return here once they read that transport has blown?"

"I do, Kelis." Stag had considered it at length. "They'll probably believe the woman activated the bomb and the cargo section possibly survived, or that some of crates managed to avoid destruction. They have an interest in the bots. I just wish we could have taken all of them. Any use they have for those models wouldn't bode well for anyone."

"They'd probably turn them into assassins. They seem to love to kill anything alive," Hellion muttered.

Stag agreed.

"I just picked something up on the sensors," Veller stated. "Either it's someone else who picked up the distress signal or the Markus Models are on their way back." He paused. "I'm picking up two ships now." His voice deepened. "Shit. They are reading as Genesis Four shuttles. It's the Markus Models."

"They likely found their brothers and are traveling at their top speed." Stag ground his teeth together. "Full burn now, and forget about trying to stay off their sensors by moving slow enough to be mistaken as space debris. They must suspect a ship is here. We can't win a battle with two S-class shuttles. They're faster and maneuver better than the *Varnish*. Take us out of range, change course, and find cover."

"On it," Hellion rasped. "I don't like running from them. Every instinct says to fight."

Stag hated it too. "We're outnumbered, and our mission was to locate the Markus Models and set out trackers. It's going to take more than just the *Varnish* to destroy their shuttles. Patience will win this war."

Tension filled the control room as they all watched the sensors. They made it out of range of tracking, which meant the Markus Models couldn't be seen either. Veller spoke first.

"I found cover."

"Where?" Stag leaned forward in his chair.

"A cluster of four moons." He tapped in the coordinates and displayed them for everyone.

Stag gazed at the map. "Too obvious. That's where I'd look first."

"There's not much this way except a dead zone."

Stag jerked his chin up and stared at Veller. "Dark space?"

"Affirmative. Some warning markers are up and transmitting. It's vast." Veller tapped his pad, reading something on it. "Four ships are reported lost in it. No charts are showing anything on the other side."

Stag fisted his hand. "Take us to the edge and stop."

Hellion drew his attention by cursing. "That's insane. I know what you're thinking but we can't go in there. We might not find our way out."

"The Markus Models will deem we're too smart to have entered it. They'll waste time searching those moons." Stag smiled.

"Unless they think we're Earthers." Hellion snorted.

"Exactly," Kelis agreed. "It's stupid to enter it. We'd have to go deep to avoid them visually spotting us. That means they'd lose sight of us, but we'd lose sight of where the entry point is. Our sensors will have nothing to read to pinpoint our location."

"We're cyborgs," Stag reminded his crew. "We're smarter than the Earthers who have ventured inside. We'll get out, but I'm going to send our coordinates to the *Star* just in case, with a seventy-four-hour window so they'll know to come looking for us if we don't contact them after that. The Markus Models won't waste that much time searching in this area. They'll return to whatever mission they are on or move right past us."

"They could pick up the transmission. There's only one relay in this system to send our message. It's probably why they avoided using it to contact each other."

Stag didn't need Kelis to tell him that. "It's why I'm typing out my breeding-pact lists with names. I'm number four on mine. I'm creating a code. It's too easy to break if they use a zero-to-nine numerical system."

"Smart," Hellion muttered.

"That's why I'm in charge."

Stag quickly typed out the message by using the first initial of each male on his list, to signify a number, until he had the coordinates of where they'd enter the dead zone of space. He sent it.

"Do you think they'll figure it out easily?"

"Flint is smart, and he's in charge of the *Star* right now. I titled it B.P. List, and that will clue him in." Stag sighed. "Otherwise he's an idiot but he's not one. He'll realize I'm giving him numbers. The Markus Models won't be able to break my code, Hellion."

"How will he know who is on your list and their numbers?"

Stag hated his authority being questioned. "At least three men in mine are assigned to the *Star*."

Hellion nodded. "They can decode it."

"Exactly." Stag leaned forward. "Take us into the dead zone. Count it out every second, our speed, and record how far we go before changing course. We'll just reverse and exit by using that information."

"It's going to mess with our sensors."

"I'm aware. Don't use them." He stood up, walked to the front, stared at the utter blackness they flew into. "Visuals only. Mark time and speed."

"Shit," Hellion muttered. "I get why we're doing this but I'm not happy about it."

"Turn on your emotion-suppression chip if you're going to whine." Stag had no time to deal with feelings. "I refuse to allow us to be captured by Markus Models. I'd rather us all die on our terms than be tortured for the location of other cyborgs. We have a good chance of getting out of this. Those bastards have two Genesis Four shuttles at their disposal and the *Varnish* would be no match for them. They'd take out our engines and board us. Our intel said they're traveling in units of four to six. We're not equipped for hand-to-hand combat with that many."

"It's a sound decision. The Markus Models wouldn't think we'd do this."

He turned to glance at Kelis. The male gave him a sharp nod, communicating that he was in agreement with Stag's decision.

"Maybe they'll follow us in and get lost if they enter the dead zone too." Veller grinned. "That would be a bonus."

"They are intelligent. They'd have the same odds as we do of finding the edge again."

Stag's words muted his crew. He faced forward. "Tell me when the sensors stop getting readings."

Long minutes passed. "Now," Parqel whispered.

"Visuals?"

Hellion answered. "Gone. Not a glimmer of light from the stars."

"Shutter all ports and turn off any exterior lighting." Stag returned to his chair, changing course himself. He knew his crew was watching, memorizing every order he input. He finally used the thrusters and brought the shuttle to a full stop. "We're going to become as dark as our surroundings."

"Shit," Hellion murmured.

It was eerie quiet when the engines were shut down. Stag kept life support on but at a minimum. "We wait. In seventy-two hours, we'll reverse course. I want two of you visually scanning for any lights. The Markus Models will have to rely on visuals too and might amplify their exterior lights, hoping to spot us." He tapped out a new schedule, sending it to their pads. "Rest as much as possible to slow your breathing."

"Why did you lower life support?"

Kelis answered Hellion's question first. "In case we can't find our way out. We'll use less fuel repowering our systems and survive longer in case we're stuck out here."

Stag leaned back in his chair and slowed his breathing, measuring each one. He also accessed lighting inside the ship, dimming it to draw less power. "We'll get out of this."

He hoped he hadn't just lied to his crew.

Chapter Three

Nala made the bed and glanced around the room. The lights were so low it was difficult to see much. Stag was a mega asshole for making it as tough as possible to clean his quarters, but she'd done it.

Her stomach grumbled. He'd wanted to motivate her to do his bidding, and he had. She'd been abandoned in his room for what she guessed was a good seventeen hours now. The only reason she had access to water was the cleansing unit sink.

"What a dick," she muttered.

She took a seat on the floor in case Stag was anything like her father. Manny Vestria had hated creases on his bedding. He'd spent twenty years in the military, before he'd retired and taken a job with her on her transport shuttle.

She drew her knees up and hugged them. Her father and the *Pride* were gone.

The freighter had been her baby. She'd sold everything after her grandfather's death and bought it at an auction. Some smuggler had been caught by Earth Government and his loss had become her gain. She'd hired men her dad had trusted, ex-military buddies of his, and she'd built her reputation as being honest and dependable. At first she'd landed a few jobs hauling supplies to colonies, but then she'd hit the jackpot by being given a contract to deliver sex bots.

Now she had nothing. Tears filled her eyes but she blinked them back. It was done. There was no changing the past. She'd learned that lesson from a young age. She'd been the daughter of a military officer who'd spent more time in space than on Earth. Her mother had died when she'd been eight, her grandmother four years later. Then her grandfather, when she'd been nineteen and just learning the import business he had built.

Earth Government had come in and said they were taking over the business, using the excuse that she wasn't qualified. There'd been nothing left on Earth for her at that point. She'd sold the house, emptied her grandfather's credit accounts, and bought her freighter. EG couldn't steal from her again if she wasn't living on the planet.

The door opened and she lifted her chin. Stag entered then sealed them inside. He held a covered tray. "Food."

She rose up and was tempted to hit him with the damn thing but hunger couldn't be denied. It might feel good to shove whatever he'd bought all over his nice, neat uniform but in the long run, she'd be the one to suffer for her show of defiance. He might wait another seventeen hours to feed her.

"Thank you." She accepted the tray and returned to her spot on the floor.

"You may sit on the bed."

"It's been made with clean sheets and blankets. I even fluffed your pillows." She hoped he'd smother on them. "I don't want to mess it up again."

35

He took a seat on the bed and she could feel him watching her, but she focused on the tray, lifting the lid. The smell hit her instantly and her body reacted to the delicious aroma. She grabbed a fork and dug into what passed for meatloaf, mashed potatoes, and gravy.

"I apologize for the wait. I didn't mean to stay on shift that long."

She wasn't buying his excuse but decided to not call him on it. For now, she was a prisoner, and she'd play his little control-freak game. She had no choice.

"Is this the silent treatment?"

She swallowed and stared up at him. "This is the 'I'm so hungry I'm eating this as fast as possible before you decide to take it away' treatment."

"Eat slower. I won't take it from you. The Markus Models were returning to your ship. We entered a dead zone to avoid them finding us."

Her hand froze, the fork inches from her mouth. "You what?"

"I didn't want to leave Control until I was certain we wouldn't be found. We've seen no sign of them. They weren't able to follow our trail inside."

"We're in the Pitch?"

"I'm not familiar with that term."

"The Pitch. It's what they call that black hole or dead zone, whatever. Every captain in this sector knows to avoid it. Didn't your sensors read the warning markers put up along the border? That would be an alert transmitted to your computer to not to go beyond that point or dire shit happens."

"I wasn't aware it had been named."

She put the fork down and took a drink from the cup he'd brought. The liquid tasted like red wine. It surprised her that cyborgs had some, but she didn't comment on it. It was usually a drink reserved for important celebrations. "You're crazy. Do you know how many ships have entered the Pitch and never been heard from again?"

"Four."

"Oh, it's way higher than that."

"The marker warning stated four."

"It hasn't been updated in forever then. They lost two ships just last year. Probably three the one before that. The first time I traveled out this way, a colony-seeking ship thought it would be fun times to see what might be on the other side of it. There were a hundred and nineteen souls aboard, and that was six years ago. They were never heard from again. I was told they sent in rescue ships searching for it. Over twenty went in, and they spaced them apart but close enough to keep in sight of each other, and still managed to lose six when they drifted in too far. You crazy bastard."

He frowned. "We had no choice."

"Run. How about that? You burn thrusters until they give up chasing you."

"Is that what you tried? How did that work out for you?"

37

"I didn't pick that damn shuttle up on sensors. It docked and they attacked before I knew what was happening. I would have run if I'd seen it coming."

"Are you familiar with Genesis Four S-class shuttles?"

"I've never heard of them."

"They're new, top-of-the-line, and can outrun most existing ships, especially an old freighter like yours. They are also heavily shielded to prevent damage. You would have run and they'd have caught you, boarded you anyway, and your crew would still be dead. This shuttle is faster than your freighter, and I knew they'd still catch up to us."

She lowered her gaze, taking in that information. It helped alleviate her guilt a little. It sounded as though the *Pride* had never stood a chance.

"Nala?"

She looked back at him, holding his gaze. It was impossible not to notice his good looks or how incredibly blue and vivid his eyes were.

"This was our only possibility for survival. I can't allow the Markus Models to capture any of my crew."

"You might have signed their death warrants anyway when you flew us into the Pitch."

"To avoid death wasn't my priority. We have information they can't ever obtain. Capture isn't an option."

"What kind of info?"

"Where other cyborgs are. They want to trade that information to Earth Government. Only a limited number of the Markus Models escaped, so we theorize they want to start a conflict between Earth and my kind. Earth Government would send battle cruisers to kill us, and it would make it easier for them to slip back to the planet and free more of their models once security around Earth wasn't as tight."

She held up her hand. "Stop. You're telling me androids are plotting all this? It sounds like some kind of coup."

"Yes."

"They are machines. Who programmed them? Rebels? Military?"

"It doesn't matter. They believe they are sentient but they aren't."

"I've heard that before."

He frowned again, narrowing his eyes. Anger showed on his face when a muscle in his jaw clenched. "*We* are sentient. They are not. They have hive-brain thinking, all linked together. We're individuals. We don't wish to exterminate innocent life. They believe they are the only beings worthy of existing."

"So they're control freaks?"

"They judge Earthers as inferior and kill any they find."

"Would they pretend I'm an android when I'm not one?"

He stood. "Don't insult me. I'm nothing similar to the Markus Models. They killed at least one of your crew members by dissecting him while he was still alive."

She reeled back, her stomach heaving. It was a fight to avoid throwing up the food she'd just gotten down. *God, don't ask who it was.*

39

She didn't want to know. It hadn't been her father. His body had been dressed and on the floor.

"I apologize. That was harsh. But you piss me off. Don't make accusations like that, it's a deep insult to be compared to the Markus Models."

She forced her chin up and glared at him. "So you've never killed people before?"

"Only in self-defense."

"What's your version of that, just to be clear?"

"When they attacked or meant to do us harm first."

"I guess we can agree on one thing. Our definition of that is the same."

"I'm going to shower before sleep. I've been up for nearly twenty-nine hours."

He moved past her, entered the cleansing unit, and she managed to pick at more of her food, trying to eat as much of it as her stomach would allow. It might be a while before he fed her again.

It didn't take the cyborg long to get clean, since the unit was only on for about two minutes. It opened and Nala turned her head.

Shock hit hard as he stepped out only sporting a towel wrapped around his waist. The fork clattered to the floor.

Her gaze flickered down his body, taking it all in. No hair showed on his chest. His nipples were two flat disks, darker in color. Muscles were clearly defined along the tops of his shoulders, down his hulking arms, and all along his abdomen. He had a broad upper body but his waist thinned to narrow hips, then flared out again under the short towel, displaying muscular thighs. A little bit of hair adorned his legs but not much.

He had the best body she'd ever seen, by a long shot. Sure, her crew had taken off their shirts sometimes to work when the cooling system had failed. They were all hairy, older, and she hadn't paid much attention. She couldn't exactly say that about Stag.

He might be a jerk, but he was a really hot one. He'd been designed to be attractive to the eye in every way, and the company who'd made him had been right on target. Handsome, perfect physique to attract a buyer's eye, and sleek enough that anyone with a heartbeat would want to touch him.

She lifted her gaze to his chest again. Some light scars marred his smooth skin. They looked like tiny white lines on his soft gray skin tone, some of them jagged. It took effort for her to blink and force her head to turn away. "I think you forgot to put something on," she managed to say.

"These are my quarters. I wear a uniform while I'm on shift. I enjoy relaxing when I'm alone."

"Well, I'm here, and I'd appreciate it if you could at least wear pants."

"Your desires aren't my concern."

That word hit a nerve with her. It had been six years, nine months, and thankfully she'd forgotten how many days since she'd left Earth. Add in a few more weeks before that and it was the last time she'd had a boyfriend. Most women her age had a lover, or even a few, but she'd had a crew of men her father had chosen because they were as crabby as him.

Every man she'd met at pickup and delivery sites had been chased off if they even looked at her twice. That had been the down side of working with her dad and his friends. They had been overprotective. No guy had a chance of getting near her without a laser gun pointed at him.

They'd visited stations to take breaks but her crew never allowed her go anywhere alone. She'd put her foot down on her twenty-fourth birthday and confronted her dad. It had been over four years at that point since she'd had sex. They'd both been embarrassed by the conversation, but she'd won. He'd agreed to let her to visit an automated brothel. He'd agreed sex bots were safer than letting her into a bar to pick up a real guy. It had been her bad luck that they didn't host any male bots. She'd returned to the *Pride* frustrated.

Six years since I've had sex. That's why I'm noticing he's hot. She sighed.

"Are you contemplating how to kill me?"

Nala refused to tell Stag where her thoughts had gone, instead glaring up at him. "How did you guess?"

"Your tone implies disdain."

"Give me a break. What am I going to do? Stab you with my fork? You'd just pull it out and be pissed some more. I could hit you with the tray but whatever part of you I nail would just dent the thin metal sheet. I'm not stupid. I'd break bones if I punched you. No thanks."

"Are you done eating? I'm ready to go to bed."

42

Her heart rate increased as she gave him a once-over again, her gaze lingering on his abs and that towel. After her twenty-fourth birthday, she'd secretly stashed an image advertisement for a sex bot model in her quarters. It had been blond, brown-eyed, and a bit smaller bodied than the cyborg in front of her.

She stood up. Stag might not have the greatest personality but she could get over that if he planned to touch her. It had been a really long time since anyone had. He claimed to be sentient. It implied he might have all the right body parts. He motioned his head toward the bed.

"You get the inside."

"We're sharing?"

"Yes. I won't let you sleep on the floor. It's too hard and cold. That would be cruel."

She climbed up on the bed and lay down. He didn't follow but instead walked over to the wall of storage and opened a high panel she couldn't reach. He jerked something down that she didn't catch sight of.

"Computer, dim lights to three percent."

The room became so dark she couldn't see anything. Disappointment hit. He meant to just sleep. She closed her eyes and scooted closer to the wall. He really was a machine. Only one of those wouldn't try to seduce a woman in his bed.

The mattress dipped and the covers she lay on pulled a bit from his weight. She turned onto her side, giving him her back. He probably didn't want any part of them to touch and that meant pressing tight against the wall. It wasn't a large bed but it was wider than a single bunk.

"Give me your wrist. Raise it."

Her eyes snapped open. "Why?"

"I'm restraining you. I don't trust you not to attack me in my sleep."

"Give me a break!" She was really getting fed up with his accusations. "You're a cyborg. I'm not. How much stronger are you than a typical human? I'm guessing what? Five times?"

"Give me your wrist or I'll force it. I don't want to bruise you more."

She flung her arm up and over her head. "Paranoid bastard. There. You just want the one or both?"

"Both."

"Great. That's going to be comfy for sleeping."

"I'm more concerned with *my* comfort."

"Of course you are. Dick." She lifted the other one.

He was tender when he touched her, wrapping some soft material around each wrist. It felt a little elastic but thick. She was at least grateful he didn't use cuffs. It would have hurt to rest her wrists on metal bands as she slept. He released her and she tested the give in them. They weren't so tight she couldn't move around a bit. He'd tethered her somehow to the frame above her head, but he'd given her enough length to move her arms about a foot.

"Computer, lights at ten percent."

She twisted her head, staring at her wrists now that she could see them. "Belts?"

"Yes. From my workout gear. Don't tug hard and they won't abuse your skin."

"Do you feel safer now?" She stared at him under her upraised arm. He lay on his side, facing her.

"I do."

"Fantastic."

He reached over her waist, upward, and tapped a finger on the wall. A hidden compartment sprang open. He withdrew a folded cloth and a small black bottle.

Fear hit. "Don't you dare drug me."

He made a sound like a snort and closed the panel. "Go to sleep. This isn't for you."

He rolled onto his back and she laid her head down, wondering if he drugged himself to sleep. Barney, one of her crew, used that method, pouring his sleep medicine into a rag and breathing it in when insomnia bothered him.

The bed shifted a bit and she heard the distinctive sound of something hitting the floor. It sounded suspiciously like his towel.

Did the cyborg sleep totally naked on top of the covers? She was right next to him. Maybe he hadn't been taught how rude and inappropriate that was. Cyborgs might not regard nudity the same way people did.

The next noise was the cap of the bottle being popped open. Curiosity pricked at her over what he was doing but she refused to give in

45

to the need to peek. She wasn't going to ask why he used drugs. It wasn't any of her business.

Nala tried to relax, hoping to sleep since it wasn't as if she had been given a choice. She adjusted her cheek, resting it on the inside of her arm for a pillow.

The mattress moved, and she frowned, wondering what Stag was doing now.

Then the bed rocked a little bit. A new sound came with the motion, a slightly wet one. *What the hell?*

She couldn't take it anymore and opened her eyes, turned her head, and lifted up a bit to get a look at him.

Stag lay flat on his back less than a foot from her. The cloth was spread out on his lower stomach and upward, almost to his rib cage. One of his hands was firmly wrapped around his very stiff cock.

Her eyes widened, watching his hand move up and down his sex as he arched his hips. He had been created with all the appropriate anatomy of a man. The shaft was thick and long, the head fuller, and it glistened in the light. That was the source of the sound. It wasn't a drug in the bottle, but some kind of lotion or lube.

"What are you doing?" The words burst out of her before she could stop them.

He didn't stop or even slow down manipulating his dick with his hand. "Quiet. I'm almost ready to come. Don't ruin the moment for me."

She twisted her head away, squeezed her eyes closed, and her heart pounded. Stag was jacking off right next to her.

46

Her entire body turned rigid. She'd never seen anyone do that before, but the seconds she'd witnessed his fist pumping his cock were burned into her memory. His skin was a light gray but it was darker on his sex. His breathing increased in pace, becoming choppier, and then he groaned. The bed jerked when his body did. The motion stopped for long seconds.

"Now I can sleep."

She startled when he pressed up against her back, and she opened her eyes, watching him reach up to drop the cloth and bottle back into the hidden drawer, then push it closed. He rolled away, no longer touching her.

Time passed and she started to relax again. She had almost drifted to sleep when Stag rolled into her, curling his big body against hers. Her eyes popped open, staring at the wall, wondering what he'd do to her.

"I'm not a machine," he rasped, close to her ear. One of his hands wrapped around her waist, then slid upward. She sucked in a sharp breath when his fingers pressed over her breast. He just rested them there. "I'm also not a sex bot, or I'd have gotten *you* off, instead of myself."

She swallowed and didn't say a word. He had to know she was wide awake now. He moved his hand, slid it down her stomach slowly, and paused over her belly button.

"I'd have either used my fingers or mouth to make you come, then I'd have fucked you." He slid his hand upward again, and that time, firmly cupped her breast, massaging it through the thin material.

47

She gasped. It didn't hurt. She wished it did but her body responded to his husky voice, the things he said, and the way he closed two of his fingers, lightly pinching her nipple between them. It had been far too long since she'd been touched to be immune. The fact that he was so attractive didn't help.

"You have a beautiful body. I wanted you the first moment I saw you." He jerked her against his firm, long length, spooning to her back tightly. He was warm and had her trapped between his arm and chest. "We could have shared a lot of pleasure...except you're an Earther." He released her and rolled away. "Go to sleep."

Nala closed her eyes and forced her breathing to slow. "You really are a bastard."

"You're learning," he agreed. "Androids don't hold grudges—but I do."

Chapter Four

Stag couldn't get his mind off Nala. He'd managed to get some sleep but not much. It was the first time he'd shared a bed with someone else, and the circumstances hadn't been ideal. Regret kept washing through him. It was possible he'd gone too far to teach the Earther a lesson, and get a little payback at the same time.

Hellion cleared his throat, drawing his attention.

"What is it?"

The cyborg had turned in his seat in Control. "You haven't said one word in the hour since you began your shift. It's just us. How is it going with Nala?"

"I'm not discussing her."

"I'd have done my best to seduce her."

"I'm not you. Watch your screen and I'll watch mine."

"It's boring looking for any lights in all this darkness. I've felt nervous since we entered this dead zone."

Irritation rose. "Turn off your feelings."

"You always suggest that. Why?"

"Because I'm not allowed to directly order you to shut them off unless you've become a danger to yourself or others. It's annoying when you question my orders. You wouldn't do that if you weren't feeling nervous."

"Doesn't this bother you at all?"

"Hiding from the enemy? Yes. Being in a dead zone? No."

"We have no sensor readings since there's nothing for them to bounce off of. There's absolutely nothing here."

Stag stood, stretching his legs. "Watch the screen, Hellion. We *hope* there's nothing out there. The Markus Models might have followed us inside. Don't let your guard down or I'll put you on another duty."

Hellion lowered his head, his lips clamped together. Stag hated to scold his crew, but some cyborgs had become a little lax in their compliance. It was his job as commander of the *Varnish* to keep them in line.

Stag took a seat again, monitoring his own screen.

A glint flashed.

Stag reached out, zooming in on it. It was a quick ray of moving light but then it faded. He slapped his other hand down on his console.

"Everyone to Control. Now!"

Hellion twisted. "What is it?"

"Section three-six-four."

"I see nothing."

"I did, and we need to be prepared. There's something in the dead zone with us."

"Maybe it was a glitch on the screen."

The doors opened sooner than expected and Kelis rushed inside. Stag didn't reprimand him for his lack of uniform or shoes. The male wore

50

sleeping shorts and his hair was mussed from leaving his bed. He slid into his seat at weapons.

"What's going on?"

"Uncertain. I saw a flash of light." Then Stag spotted another and enlarged it on the main screen so they could all see it.

"What is that?" Kelis tried to read their sensors but nothing showed on them.

Parqel and Veller entered. They wore sparring outfits. Both of them paused, staring at the flare of light crossing the front display.

Stag amplified the camera to the max and cursed. "Maze and Yammer, report now. What are your locations?"

Neither answered. He scanned life signs, finding both of them inside their quarters. Both males had to be sleeping not to answer his hail. They'd had the last shift.

He locked their doors, his mind working fast to take over functions on his ship.

"Belt in," he ordered his men. "They are blindly firing, hoping to hit us."

He overrode the computer in his quarters, turning on the coms. "Nala? Brace for possible impact. Do you hear me?"

He heard her gasp. "What's happening?"

"The lowest wall panel under the bunk is where the survival equipment is kept. Prepare for hull breaches."

"What's going on?"

51

He cut her off, focusing on removing the oxygen from all nonessential areas near the exterior of the shuttle. The damage would be lessened if they sustained a hit. He used thrusters, turning the ship to make them a smaller target.

Another flare of light showed on the screen, closer to them.

"Can we move to where we've already seen lights?" Veller's low voice revealed his tension.

"There is no pattern. I'm watching for one," Stag admitted. "They could broadside us if we attempt to move where they've already fired."

"I can't believe they've waited out there all this time." Hellion shot nervous looks to the others. "What if they're still waiting when we hit our exit time?"

"Let's worry about the here and now." Stag overrode the coms in Maze's and Yammer's quarters, informing them what was going on. Both men responded, now awake. He ordered them to stay where they were and released the locks on their rooms so they could get out if severe damage happened in their area.

"Incoming," Veller warned.

Stag adjusted thrusters, avoiding the flare of light. It missed but they got a better look at what the Markus Models were firing at them. "Smart bastards."

Hellion had a wordier reaction. "Son of a bitch. Those are rigged to come apart on impact and the mini bombs inside are attracted to metals. They might have reprogrammed them to just open and deploy at certain distances."

52

"We can hope there's nothing near us to hit." Kelis kept calm. "The range on them is about forty meters once the load is dispersed. That one passed us and is out of range."

"They've effectively mined the area with bombs that will be attracted to the *Varnish* if we pass any deployed ones." Stag watched for more of the weapons. "All the ones I've seen have flown beyond range. That's good."

"What if they opened some of them ahead of us?" Veller sent the visuals from his personal pad to the main screen to show them where the *Varnish* was, and where he estimated they had come from when they'd entered the dead zone. "We have to pass through this path to reverse our course."

Stag agreed it wasn't the best news. But it could have been worse. They didn't spot any more flares, but that only meant the thrusters on the missiles weren't active. Stag forced his body to relax.

"We'll wait, watch, and prepare for our exit."

"What do you have in mind?" Kelis turned his chair, staring at Stag.

"Decoys. We'll move slow and shoot metal objects ahead of us. The bombs will be drawn to them and attach."

"The *Varnish* is a much larger mass than any small objects we can fire ahead of us."

Stag was aware of that. "The only other option is to blast out of here at full burn and hope we don't fly directly into one. We'd pass them at too high a rate of speed for them to be able to attach to our hull."

"They'd turn when they sensed us, but we'd be out of range before they could lock on." Hellion nodded. "Even direct impacts might not make them detonate. There is a two-second delay. We could be past them with enough speed." He smiled. "I like that plan better."

Stag wasn't fond of either option. Both had problems. The slow way might mean suffering massive damage to the ship, but the fast way could make leaving the dead zone more difficult. At full burn, they might make miscalculations on their exit. "Watch your screens."

He relayed the options to the two crew in their quarters, ordering them to try to return to sleep. He didn't notify Nala. He wanted her on alert in case something went wrong. Cyborgs could react faster. Her reflexes would be slower and she wasn't as tough to kill.

It bothered him, thinking of something happening to her.

He shoved his thoughts away, focusing on his task. They watched for more flaring but no lights showed in the vast darkness around them.

* * * * *

Nala sat on the bed with an oxygen canister and mask within reach. Time had dragged by since Stag's voice had cut into her sleep. His warning had woken her and she'd discovered he'd left to go on shift, and that he'd freed her wrists. The drawer he'd told her about did hold emergency equipment in case of a ship failure. She wouldn't suffocate, and she now had a med kit, as well as a temperature suit to keep her from freezing if life support went down.

So far nothing bad had happened. No explosions had been heard or felt.

Hours passed.

She had used the cleansing unit, taking her portable oxygen with her, and then explored Stag's storage drawers. Some refused to open at her touch, unauthorized to her, but she'd found more of her clothes. She'd chosen a tunic and casual pants. She even put on a pair of his socks to protect her feet in case of catastrophe.

She got up and paced. It was her job to be in charge. After six years, she was the one used to giving orders. "This sucks! I hate feeling helpless."

The door opened and she was actually glad to see the grim but handsome cyborg as he returned to his quarters.

"Situation?"

He let the door close behind him and bent, tearing off his boots. "Don't you have a bed to make?" He glanced at it. "I'm in need of a nap."

"Bullshit. What happened? What's going on?" A suspicion crossed her mind. "Did you lie just to freak me out? That would be all kinds of messed up, Stag. Cruel even. I've been worried sick and just waiting for shit to hit the fan."

"You can call me master. It has a nice ring to it, from an android."

"You bastard. Stop with that crap!" Her temper blew. "I'm right, aren't I? You wanted me afraid and thinking we were in some dire situation just to get even because you're still mad at me for some stupid reason!" She wanted to beat on him, even it would be a wasted effort.

55

She stormed to the bed, and gripped the small tank. She threw it at his chest.

He caught it with ease, showing off his reflexes. "No, I didn't lie to you. We're in a 'situation', as you called it. The alert is ongoing." He walked over to her and offered the tank. "Keep that close. You might still need it."

She tried to calm herself but it was hard. It was like he was *trying* to make her furious. She glanced down at the tank, then back up at him. "I don't believe you."

"It's not a requirement. I don't want you to die, so take this. I can hold my breath for over two minutes to reach another canister. You can't, nor are you able to reach where another one is located." He offered it again by pushing it against her chest.

She took the tank and tossed it on the mattress, not taking her gaze off him. He seemed actually concerned for her ability to survive. That was something. "What do you want me to say? Sorry I compared you to a sex bot? You're a cyborg. Excuse me if the information I heard isn't right. Couldn't you take it as a compliment that I thought you were sexy and said I wanted to buy you?"

One eyebrow arched.

"Do you know how much a sex bot costs? I do. Four hundred and twenty-five thousand credits. Do you know what I clear a year after paying out my crew and for fuel, repairs, and docking fees? Just over a hundred thousand." She fisted a handful of hair. "See this? Do you know why I've grown it so long? Some weirdo I deal with frequently offered to pay me fifty thousand credits if I'd grow it three feet and sell it to him. It was a compliment, *Stag*." She said his name on purpose. "People really have to want a sex bot bad to go to all this trouble to own one. Be flattered!"

His eyebrow lowered and his eyes narrowed. He didn't say a word though.

"What? Why are you looking at me like that?"

"Did you plan to buy a bot for your own use?"

Damn. She'd said too much. She glanced around, not able to hold his stare as she lied and backed away from him. "No. Of course not. I'm just saying, I haul them in my cargo hold. I know what they cost, and they aren't cheap." She stopped and looked at him again. "I'd say thanks if some guy thought I was a bot and wanted to buy *me*."

That was a fib too. She'd have decked someone for thinking he could pay her *any* price for sex, human or bot. Her hair was for sale, but not the rest of her body.

He moved fast, and she gasped when he grabbed her. One of his arms locked around her waist, the other one cupping her head. He pressed her up against the nearest wall, pinning her there with his body.

He adjusted her so they were eye level and he peered at her with a scowl. "You're lying. Don't do that."

He scared her. He was strong, fast, and held her off her feet as if she were as light as the pillow on his bed. She calmed fast though, when it sank in that he hadn't hurt her. The arm around her waist wasn't

57

squeezing too tight and the back of his hand had hit the wall, not her skull. He'd used it to cushion her from impact with the solid object.

"I *hate* deceit. This is why I never trust Earthers. It's all your kind does. They manipulate and twist facts. Do you want me to tell you all the ways I can detect a lie from you?"

She licked her lips and took a deep breath, unable to look away from the blue depths of his eyes. They were dazzling. "Fine. I admit it. I've been saving for a Dax 333 since my twenty-fourth birthday. Happy? All the brothels on our travel routes only cater to men. They don't buy male bots."

He smiled.

"I so don't like you."

"Why a bot and not an Earther? You could have one of those for free. You're attractive. Any man would have sex with you if you showed an interest."

"That's none of your business."

He shifted his body, spread his legs, and pinned her tighter to the wall. "Are you comfortable? I'm not releasing you until you answer my questions."

"Bully."

He blinked again.

She could tell he wasn't bluffing. "Do you want a list?"

"Yes."

She thought fast. "I'll make a deal with you."

"I'm not having sex with you."

Her mouth fell open. "Like I would ask you to. You don't exactly inspire me to want you." She grabbed his shoulders and tried to push him back but he didn't budge.

"What is your deal? I'm curious to hear what you want."

"I'll answer any questions you ask with total honesty from now on if you promise to drop the android bit and let me go free at the first opportunity. I want to leave your ship."

"No."

"I'm not your prisoner. I didn't do anything illegal. My freighter was attacked. You have no right to keep me on your ship by force or lock me up."

"I'll agree to cease calling you an android for your honesty, as long as you don't lie to me again, but your release isn't up for negotiation."

"Why not? You answered my distress signal. You have to take me to a station. That's the law. Survivors are transported to the nearest one and left there so they can report the incident that took place. I have an insurance carrier to notify and the authorities need to do something about those Markus Models. They murdered my dad and crew! I want them hunted down to pay for that."

"You've seen us."

"So?"

"I can't allow you to tell any other Earthers about this ship, about us, or that we're hunting the Markus Models."

59

"I hate to break this to you, but people already know about cyborgs. That's how I knew what you were on sight. Gray skin means cyborg. Nothing else was ever made like you. As for your ship, I don't know anything about it because this is the only room I've seen. I don't even know the class of it. Your stateroom is as basic as they come. The *Pride* wasn't the only vessel those things have attacked. I heard reports that they killed people on stations too. Warnings have been going out for a while now about Markus Models. I just never knew what they looked like until you told me that's what boarded us."

"No actual reports of our survival have been verified. We're keeping it that way."

He had her there. Cyborgs were all supposed to be dead. Sometimes rumors floated that there had been sightings, but the government news stated they were hoaxes. "So I won't tell them. Simple. You want me to lie and say some random crew picked me up and dropped me off at a station? Fine. I can do that. I'll tell them I was too traumatized to really notice anything about them or their ship. No problem."

"I don't trust your word."

She closed her eyes, took a few seconds to get a reign on her temper, since slapping him wouldn't help her cause. She looked at him again. "I'm motivated. Do you believe *that*? I want off this ship, and I don't ever want to give you a reason to come after me. How about that? I know you hold a grudge."

"We'll discuss your future at a later date. We're in the dead zone, so I couldn't take you to a station even if I wanted to at the moment. We're waiting out the Markus Models to avoid capture. Now—why did you want to buy a sex bot when you could have had an Earther lover without it costing you credits? The truth."

"There were a lot of reasons."

"Name them."

"My dad."

"Explain."

"He wasn't around much while I was growing up. He retired and came to work for me once I bought the freighter. Ever heard of that saying 'making up for lost time'? It fit. He was really overprotective. Men couldn't look at me without him drawing a weapon. He didn't trust them not to hurt me."

"By forcing sex?"

"That too. He was also worried they'd give me a disease or worse."

"Abuse you?"

"Do you know what real women in brothels are worth, this deep in space? I do. My dad constantly told me. He was terrified some guy was going to trick me into trusting him, kidnap me, and sell me on the black market."

"It happens."

"I know. I hear the news too. It's partly why I decided to buy a bot. They're programmed not to hurt humans, they don't carry diseases, and my dad wouldn't want to shoot it because it doesn't have an ulterior motive. He'd consider it safe...and I'd have had company."

"You had a crew and your father. It wasn't a large freighter. You weren't alone."

"Can you put me down?"

He eased her onto her feet and released her. She slid along the wall and moved around him to put space between them. "Thank you. And I may as well have been." She took a seat on the bed.

He turned, watching her.

"They were all my dad's age or older. All ex-military. What did I have in common with them? They were always talking about the past. It was a struggle to even get them to take orders from me. I'd give them, and they'd glance at my dad. He'd nod and then they'd do what they were told. I was just a kid to them. How is that for honesty? But I knew I could trust them. They weren't going to slit my throat to steal my freighter or the cargo.

"I spent most of my hours working or in my quarters alone. My dad didn't like me hanging with his friends in our down time. I think he was afraid they'd stop viewing me as his baby girl and see me as a woman. He'd have killed anyone who thought about touching me. Not that I was interested. Dad not only picked the crew because he trusted them, but they had some pretty gross habits. So not sexy to see men spitting and hearing them sharing the graphic details of past sexual encounters with whores. Denny even had the crawl and refused to take care of it. Don't get me started on how disgusting that is."

"I'm not familiar with that term."

"Some people get very dry skin on ships, and it begins to crack and peel if they don't coat the affected areas on a regular basis to protect it from happening. There's not enough moisture in the air with life support. It dries them out. Get it? Denny had the worst case of it I've ever seen, because he refused to use the medicine. It spreads if you let it go. He'd just randomly start bleeding if he moved wrong, breaking open a scab. He had a bunch of them."

Stag curled his lip in disgust.

"Exactly. Any more questions about why I wouldn't get involved with someone on my freighter?"

He approached her and sat a few feet away on the bed. "Why did you want to own the *Pride*?"

"My dad always told me stories about his space adventures when I was growing up. I realize now he embellished a lot but it sounded so exciting. Plus, unlimited opportunities for growth in business. Not like on Earth. I could make as much as I wanted, as long as I put the time and effort into it. Why did you want to be in charge of *this* ship?"

"I'm a natural leader."

She smirked. "You *are* a control freak. We're being honest, remember? It should go both ways."

A ghost of a smile played at his lips. "I enjoy giving orders more than taking them."

"Who doesn't?"

They stared at each other. She spoke first. "I'm sorry for the sex-bot thing, okay? You're a person. I'm clear on that now."

"I won't call you an android again. Unless you lie to me."

She held out her hand. "Truce?"

He glanced down at her offered gesture, then rose to his feet. "That would imply we're not enemies. You're an Earther, and I know better than to trust you."

She fisted her hand and put it on her lap. "I don't know what someone else did to you, but I'm not them. You understand that, don't you?"

"It's in your nature to be treacherous."

"You've treated me badly since we met, and yet I'm still willing to give *you* the benefit of the doubt. The only reason you saved me was because you were angry. Am I wrong?"

He just stared at her.

"I'm grateful to be alive. I'm going to focus on that." She stood. "Come on, meet me halfway. We're stuck together for a while. We can at least try to be pleasant to each other until you let me go, when you can."

"You're never going to be let go. Once we leave the dead zone, I'll hand you over to other cyborgs. They'll find you a place in our society and make certain you can't ever contact other Earthers to share the information you've acquired about us."

She regretted getting up, wishing she were still sitting. "What are you talking about?"

"You heard me. Don't be obtuse. You were saved by cyborgs, and now you'll live in our society. The life you knew is gone forever. That's the price of living. Now, prepare to have your wrists tied so I don't have to worry about you attempting to harm me while I sleep."

Nala wanted to deck him. She spun away before he could see the rage he caused. He'd not only just dashed any hope of being set free, but they were right back to square one.

If he wanted a fight, he would get one. She'd make him want to drop her off at the first space station they passed.

Chapter Five

Stag felt better after a solid six hours of sleep. He'd released Nala before he'd left his quarters. She hadn't said a word and avoided eye contact. That was fine with him. Their conversation had unsettled him. He'd almost forgotten what she was and where she came from.

Yammer stretched his arms upward and yawned. "This is tedious."

"Would you prefer we were under attack?"

The male turned, lowering his arms, and gave Stag an odd look. "You're in a sour mood. I had hoped having a female in your bed would help with your disposition."

"I'm not having intercourse with that Earther."

"A shame," Maze stated from his seat. "She's attractive. A little on the short side, and compact, but I would be pleased to share quarters with her."

"So would I," Yammer agreed. "I think she's the perfect size. She doesn't take up much room. Our bunks are small for two to share."

That *was* a problem, Stag concluded. None of his crew members were joined into a family unit, and they didn't have access on a regular basis to a female. It seemed anyone would do. They were even willing to overlook their past experiences with Earthers if it meant having a warm body under them.

"Perhaps we can keep one of the bots onboard."

Yammer almost fell out of his seat as he twisted around again, staring at Stag with a glint in his eye. "For us to use?"

"Your lack of physical stimulation is affecting your judgment. A bot won't slit your throat or betray us. An Earther would."

Yammer frowned. "You've got the female in lockdown inside your room, no access to coms, and I'm certain you've safeguarded against her getting her hands on anything that can be used as a weapon. She's not a threat."

"She would be if you became lax enough to trust her. She'd plot a way to cause harm. That's what they do. How could you forget that?"

Yammer faced forward. "True."

Maze shook his head. "I disagree."

"You're a medic. You're prone to dealing with the weak and injured, not security threats and how to manage them."

"How do you manage the Earther?"

Stag considered his answer to Maze carefully before speaking. "I saved her life. I'm responsible for her well-being until we return to Garden. I'll keep watch over her, feed her, and make certain she stays healthy. Then she will be handed over to the council and they will decide where to place her."

"We're not technically supposed to rescue Earthers. Why did you?" Maze stared at him. "It's out of character for you."

"She had information about the Markus Models, and we'd boarded her ship as part of our mission to investigate their attacks. I am confident the council won't have a problem with us taking her aboard the *Varnish*, as opposed to leaving her there to die. She *is* a female."

"It might have upset a few of the council members when they read our reports, if we'd left her to die, since some are joined in family units with Earthers." Yammer glanced at Maze. "It was a logical choice. I don't want to be reprimanded by them. It's better to err on the side of caution these days, with all the recent changes."

"That was my determination," Stag stated. It wasn't completely true. He *would* have left Nala behind, it could have been too dangerous to his own men to save her, but she'd infuriated him. He'd made the extra effort.

It angered him that he felt compelled to be dishonest with his crew. It was *her* fault. She was already corrupting him.

He couldn't wait to get out of the dead zone and hand the Earther over to the council. They could worry about placing her in a low-security job and finding her living arrangements.

Maze seemed to be thinking about her future as well when he spoke.

"The council will assign her to a male. She will need to be housed with and guided by one. I'm going to ask to be that male. She has already met me, and I'm a medic. I'd be a perfect candidate."

The thought of Maze with Nala didn't sit well with Stag. Maze would attempt to seduce her. He carefully studied the cyborg. She might find him attractive. All cyborgs had been made from what Earthers considered superior genes, for health, physical wellness, and looks.

He clenched his teeth and dropped his focus to his pad on the arm of his chair, monitoring dark space, forcing himself to focus on the task at hand.

Maze was a fool if he allowed an Earther into his home. He'd regret it. She'd betray his trust in some way. They always did.

An alarm blared and he quickly read what had caused it.

Something had attached to the hull.

He barely hit the coms in time. "Brace!"

A small explosion came from the port side. He kept calm as he took in the damage readings from the ship's sensors. It wasn't as bad as it could have been. One panel near a maintenance access had suffered a rupture but the hull under it held. He locked down that section, making certain none of his crew were in that area. He vented out the oxygen to the surrounding area so there wouldn't be a pressure issue.

"Eject some of our solar panels," he ordered.

"Decoys in case of other bombs?" Yammer did it. "Brilliant."

Stag rose from his chair. "I'm going to have to do an exterior examination and patch."

Yammer rose. "I'll do it."

Stag stared into the male's eyes. "There are bombs near us. We're aware of that now. Parts of our suits might draw them or be breached by small shrapnel if the solar panels are blown apart. We can't go to full burn with an exposed section, even if it was small. It's too risky. The hull in that section might have suffered fractures. I'll do it."

69

"You're our commander. I'm not vital."

"You are in charge."

"Stag." The cyborg gripped his arm. "It should be one of us."

"I'm not losing a member of my crew. You're in charge." He jerked out of Yammer's hold and stormed out of the room.

He was going to have to suit up and exit the shuttle, float out there and do a patch. They were at a full stop but those bombs were a severe danger. He hadn't lost a man yet—and never planned to. If one of them had to die, it would be him.

Maze caught up with him at the lift. The doors opened, and Veller and Kelis faced him. "Yammer is at the helm. I'm going outside."

"We read the damage." Kelis stepped back against the wall of the lift. "I'll repair it."

"Go to Control now. I have this," Stag ordered.

"I'm going to monitor, and be suited up to retrieve you if there's a problem."

Stag glared at Maze.

"It's my job. I'm the medic. I can overrule your orders. Kelis and Veller are here to assist Yammer. They don't need me, but you might."

Stag gave a sharp nod, then addressed the two other members of his crew. "Move."

Both males exited the lift and rushed to Control. Stag entered the lift and Maze joined him. They went to the engine section and got the patches and equipment Stag would need. Stag decided to exit out a docking bay, and suited up. Maze did as well.

"You're to stay inside."

"Understood, but the repair would go faster if two of us worked together."

"No, Maze. You are not to follow me out there. We both know I wouldn't survive if a bomb attaches to me."

"Let me go instead."

Stag put on his helmet and turned on coms. "No."

"I know what you're doing."

"Good. Hellion annoys me with his constant need for clarifications."

"I'm the least-needed member of our crew. No one is hurt. I should be the one to risk."

Stag wasn't about to waste more time arguing with the male. "How much float time have you incurred in the past five years? Answer." He already knew. Maze was *his* medic and had been assigned to him during that time.

Maze paused in putting on his suit. "None, but I've done it in the past."

"On the *Star*. You were occasionally assigned visual-inspection duty when it isn't grounded on Garden for repairs. This is different. I'm going to be working with a fusion wand to seal the patches. They can melt your suit if you're not careful of the intense heat. I did this two years ago when we took a rock hit on a thruster. Stand down on this, Maze. That's an order."

Maze put on his helmet. "I'll come after you if you're hurt. Try to be aware of what is behind you. Can I turn on the exterior lighting in that section? It will help you see better and possibly avoid one of those bombs."

"No." Stag turned on the helmet lighting. "It would be too bright and we don't know if the Markus Models entered the dead zone with us. I won't do anything to give away our location to them." He stepped into metallic boots, taking over the suit controls, and sealed the legs of the pants to the boots. "Decompressing. You ready?"

"Yes." Maze gripped a handle and locked his own boots on, sealing them to the floor.

"Close the door after me. Don't leave it open."

"I could get to you faster."

"Seal the door!" He was pissed as he hit the red button to shut off gravity in the small room. He turned, adjusted his boots, making sure he wouldn't float from the floor. He gripped the two cases he needed, hooked them together, and clipped them to a line on his suit. The lights flashed red and then went solid red. The air was gone to the room, as well as all gravity.

Stag opened the docking doors and moved forward. He hated going outside but it could have been worse. At least the shuttle wasn't in motion. He exited his ship, grabbed a handle on the hull, reaching for another one. He glanced back as the docking doors sealed. Maze had remained inside and had followed his order.

He looked forward, climbing the shuttle. The cases trailed behind him, the slight tug at his waist comforting where they were attached to the line.

* * * * *

Nala felt trepidation when the doors opened but it wasn't Stag who stepped inside.

She stood up and her body tensed. She didn't like the way the cyborg openly stared at her chest, then lower.

He held out a tray. "Food."

She was leery of approaching him. "Stag usually brings it to me."

"He's busy."

"What was that alarm I heard?"

"We experienced some small damage. Stag is repairing it."

She walked forward and accepted the tray, then retreated. She wasn't willing to turn her back on him. He was a man, and she'd learned from Stag that they had all their body parts. That made him potentially dangerous. "What kind of damage?"

"It requires an exterior patch."

She trembled. That was bad. It was a fear to anyone in space. A breach could buckle an entire section of hull if it wasn't patched fast, cause a chain reaction and take out other parts of a ship. "How? Metal fatigue?"

"No." He leaned against the doorway, still taking her in from head to foot.

"I'm Nala." She twisted and put the tray on the bed. "You are?"

"Parqel. We met before on your ship for a brief moment."

"Sorry. I don't really remember much of that." So he'd seen her naked. That made her even more uncomfortable.

"You did seem a little disorientated. How are you now?"

"Better. So Stag is out there fixing it?" That was dangerous. If the section near the breach blew, he could be killed. She was pretty sure the engines were off. There were no vibrations at all that she could feel. It meant he wouldn't float off at least, and possibly tear his suit if he were struck by any part of the ship.

"Yes. He always insists it's his life placed in danger in these situations. He's a good commander. I'm sure you did the same for your crew."

She would have, if her father had allowed it. He hadn't. "Thanks for the food."

He didn't budge. "I wanted to discuss something with you." He glanced at her chest again then met her gaze. "You're attractive."

The fear increased. He was a cyborg. Big. Strong. Enhanced. What if he attacked her? She wouldn't be able to fight him off. It was best to be polite and hope he remained the same. "Thank you."

74

"When you're taken off this ship, a male will be assigned to care for you. I'd like you to consider me. I have a good temperament. I'd be willing to transfer my duties to remain with you. Stag always assigns single males. I won't be permitted to return to this duty if you accept me."

"I'm not really sure what that means."

He pushed off the wall but didn't come any closer. "You will be given to a male to live with. He'll be in charge of your care. You won't be allowed to live on your own. We could test our compatibility."

"I also don't know what *that* means. You mean like, see if we'd make good roommates?"

He took a step closer. "Sexual compatibility. No male would live with you and not demand you give him access to your body. I would like to have intercourse, and show you that it would be a good match between us."

Nala backed up and bumped against the bed. Then she moved again, getting away from him, in case it gave him ideas. "No, but thank you for the offer."

He frowned.

"Look, you're attractive. I won't lie. But I get to know people by talking to them. I don't have sex with strangers. Understand?"

"You will be assigned to a male, and the only one you have had conversations with is Stag. He'll never offer to keep you. He hates Earthers."

"I'm aware."

"He doesn't want you. He's made that clear. I'm a good choice. Are you concerned about your upkeep? I would never abuse you."

Upkeep? She swallowed. "Let me think about it, okay? I do that. I need to let things sink in. I didn't know I'd be given to someone. You people know I'm not an android, right? That's just bullshit Stag said because I made him mad."

"You're an Earther. You can't live alone. That's how it will be. Other males will make the offer. I want you to consider me. I could show you how I would pleasure you." He took another step closer.

"No." He might be bigger but she'd still put up a fight if he tried to get her out of her clothes. "Please leave."

He took a step back. "I didn't mean to frighten you. That wasn't my intention."

"I need time to think. Alone. Thank you for the food."

He inclined his head. "I'd take good care of you. Consider me." He spun, left, and the door sealed behind him.

Nala walked to the bed and collapsed, relieved he hadn't assaulted her.

Anger came next. She was to be given away to some cyborg as though she were an android. Worse, a sex bot, since Parqel made it clear she'd be viewed as one by anyone except Stag.

She glanced at the food but it held no appeal. She'd lost her appetite.

Some cyborg would collect her when she was taken off Stag's ship and he'd demand she have sex with him. She'd seen some sex slaves on

Belton Station. They were women who'd committed crimes there and been sentenced for at least a year of servitude. The highest bidders would buy them and they'd have no choice but to comply or more time was added to the sentence.

There were rules to be followed. The men couldn't beat or maim the women. They also couldn't make a profit by leasing out rights to her body to other men. The women had to be fed, housed, and clothed. Nala had pitied them. They were forced to sleep with the men who bought them, cook for them and clean their homes. It seemed that would be her fate.

"I didn't even commit a crime," she muttered. "My freighter was attacked. This is bullshit!"

Tears came next. It was all Stag's fault. He could drop her off at some station and set her free, but he'd already sworn he wouldn't. She wiped her eyes and got up, entered the cleansing unit, and just stood there.

"What am I going to do?"

She got tissues and blew her nose, washed her face, and returned to the bed. She ignored the tray, unmotivated to try to choke it down. She was too upset.

"Damn you, you cold-hearted bastard."

Chapter Six

The doors opened and Nala bolted to her feet at the sight of two cyborgs. They carried Stag between them.

She grabbed the tray as they entered, moving it off the bed. She'd wanted to kill him, but seeing him limp, and bandages covering his shoulder, forehead, and one leg below his knee, made her instantly horrified.

"What happened? Is he okay?"

Maze and the bulky cyborg put Stag on the bed. Maze turned to her as he straightened. "There was an accident."

A third cyborg entered carrying a large med kit. He set it down, glanced at Nala, then left.

The thick-chested cyborg smiled at her. It looked a little strained. "I'm Hellion. Pick me."

"What?"

"Not now," Maze snapped. "Go. I've got this. Someone has to make sure the patch is complete and do an exterior check to see if any more damage was done."

Hellion nodded, flashed another smile at Nala—then shocked her by turning at the door, lifting his hand, and blowing her a kiss.

The doors shut, blocking her view of him, and she turned as Maze dropped to his knees next to the bed and opened the case.

"How bad is he hurt?" She evaluated Stag. He only wore the black underwear he seemed to like. His skin looked a bit off, paler than usual. "Is he going to be okay?"

Maze yanked out a scanner, a smaller one than he'd used on Nala, and ran it over Stag's head. "I patched him as best as I could inside the docking bay." He laid the scanner down and grabbed an injector, programming it with an efficiency that spoke to his knowledge of the equipment. "The leg and shoulder wounds are superficial. It's his brain I'm concerned about." He injected Stag with some kind of medication.

"What happened?"

"A bomb attached to one of our solar panels blew. It sent shrapnel toward Stag and ruptured his suit. He managed to halt the leakage but lost too much oxygen before I could get to him. It also slammed him hard into our ship. It could have been worse."

Ruptured suit? Loss of oxygen? Those were both usually causes of death. "How?"

"He didn't float off. He wedged his arm into one of the travel handles before he lost consciousness. It would have taken me more time to retrieve him otherwise."

"How long did he go without oxygen?" She noticed that Stag's chest rose and fell but that didn't mean he'd be okay. He could have suffered brain death.

"It took me three minutes and forty-two seconds to bring him in. Another thirty-two seconds to reinstate life support in the docking bay.

Add in at least sixty seconds to clear him of his helmet, open his suit, and revive him."

"Did he wake up? Say anything? Was there any air left in the suit?"

Maze grabbed the scanner, slowly running it over Stag's head again. "He was down to four percent but he'd stopped breathing by the time I was able to work on him."

That information hit Nala hard. No one could survive that long out in space if they weren't breathing. He'd have suffered brain death. Her knees almost gave out and she bent, grabbing the end of the bed.

She was so sure she hated Stag...but the pain in her chest said otherwise.

"I had to turn off all his implants when I ran an electrical current through him to restart his heart rhythm. They will be down for hours, since I had to force the shutoff. I'm not reading any real damage, so we'll have to wait."

"English," she got out.

Maze glanced at her. "That *was* in English."

"I don't know what that means!" She was upset and frustrated. "Is he brain dead? Just tell me."

"I'm reading some activity. It would be easier if I could access his chips, but I panicked."

She just stared at him, confused.

"I'm a medic. Every cyborg in my care has allowed me a pathway to hack access to their bodies in emergency situations like this one. I can shut down their implants and chips. Otherwise, sending a current of electricity through them can damage those cybernetics permanently. Stag matters too much to me, and I think I may have drained the power to them completely."

She tried to make sense of it. "I get that electrocuting them is bad, but power drain?"

Maze twisted, grabbed another scanner, and ran this one over Stag's chest. "Our bodies generate power for our cybernetic components. As a medic, I was designed to be able to drain that power to care for other cyborgs if they give me access to do so. I think I overdid it. I panicked. I wasn't calm. It means it's going to take hours for his cybernetics to recharge enough to work again."

"What does that matter? I mean, how would they help you figure out what's wrong with him?"

"We have three chips implanted inside our brains. They could tell me if there's any damage around them. They're off, and not responding to me trying to turn them back on. Recharging." He grabbed another injector, pressing it against Stag's side.

"What was that for? Is something wrong with his heart or lungs?"

"I'm not reading any damage to his organs. I just gave him a sedative to keep him under."

"Don't we *want* him to wake up?"

"He'll heal faster if he's immobile."

She felt frustrated. "If he survives."

Maze finally put his gadgets away and closed the case. He stood. "He's a cyborg. We're tough, and we heal faster than you do. It's how we were designed. I *am* reading brain function."

That calmed her. "So he's going to be fine?"

"He was lucky. The drug will keep him down for an hour. I'm going to give you access to direct coms with me. Just press your hand on the panel next to the wall and say my name. I have to go. Another crew member will leave the ship to check Stag's work on the patch and seek out any other damage. I want to be there in case there's another medical emergency. Will you watch over Stag and contact me if he's in distress?"

"I don't have much experience with injured people. How will I know?"

Maze walked over to the door and pressed his hand on the panel. "Just contact me if you become alarmed with anything. Watch him." He pulled his palm off the sensor. "The computer will now transfer your calls to me. Just say my name. It's Maze, if you've forgotten."

She nodded. "Okay."

He regarded her with a stern look. "I'm trusting you not to do him more harm. I'd have put him in my room to heal, but I hate to leave him alone in case his condition worsens. He saved your life when we took you off the *Pride*. It wasn't in our orders to save anyone on that ship. Just to investigate if it was in fact the Markus Models that had attacked it, and to see if we could gain any information of why they would target it."

"I'm not going to hurt him."

He continued to watch her.

"I swear. He's an asshole, I won't lie. But I've seen some good qualities about him too. I don't want him to die."

That seemed to alleviate any of his doubts because his expression softened. "Stag *is* a good male. He's been emotionally damaged by Earthers. It's impossible to forget the abuse we suffered while they were in control of our lives." He picked up the case. "There's a med kit in the lower bunk wall drawers. Can you wash the blood off him and redress the wounds? I sanitized them but I didn't have time to do that."

She nodded. "I can handle that."

"I'll check in when I have time. It will be a while though." He left.

Nala turned, staring at Stag. He still looked too pale, and she knew he'd hate being vulnerable to her, since she wasn't tied to the bed while he slept. She bent, crawled under the bunk, opened the drawer, and slid out the med kit, placing it by his feet at the end of the bed. A trip to the cleansing unit and she returned with warmed, wet clothes.

"Look, we might fight a lot, but I want you to wake up and be okay."

She removed the hastily applied bandage below his knee with care, his skin warm to the touch. The cut made her wince. It was jagged, about an inch long, but not deep. It wasn't actively bleeding anymore but she didn't expect it to be. Sanitizing wounds meant it hadn't only been cleaned out, but the injured blood vessels had been sealed.

She sat on the edge of the bed and gently washed away the blood from his skin, glancing up at his face. He looked younger in sleep, peaceful, and all the harsh lines that he usually wore were gone.

"Be okay, alright? I'm sure we have a ton more arguments to have before you're rid of me. Plus, if you stay the way you are, think of all the bad things I could do to you." She smiled. "I'm sure that's your biggest fear. What is that horrible Earther plotting with her devious mind?"

But her humor faded, because it was possible he'd never wake up. "You're paranoid for no reason. You haven't hurt me. We agree on the definition of self-defense, remember?"

She put a clean bandage on the wound and scooted higher, almost afraid to see what waited under the larger one on his shoulder. She placed the med kit up by his pillow, where she usually rested her head while they slept. It was tough to get close enough to him so she lifted his arm, inched closer, and laid it across her lap to lean in.

Her hands trembled a little as she used her fingernails to carefully break the seal on the bandage and lift it up. There wasn't one cut, but two. Maze said Stag had been hit with shrapnel. The medic had done more than just clean and bandage the top cut. It was deep, and she could see foam, a bonding filler that would prevent more bleeding as he healed.

"Damn, Stag," she whispered. "That had to hurt like hell." She gently cleaned around it, wondering if he needed stitches instead. Her crew would have gotten them but Stag was a cyborg. His medic would know best. She put a fresh bandage on and straightened, her gaze wandering over his stretched-out body.

His arm jerked on her lap, startling her. She looked at his face, seeing it twisted in a grimace, possibly from pain. She caressed his cheek. "Stag? It's okay. Can you hear me? You're in your room."

He groaned, and she thought he might wake, despite the sedative. That would be a good thing, in her opinion. She was concerned what the lack of oxygen had done to him.

She touched him a little more firmly, stroking his smooth skin from his jaw to his ear. "Stag? It's Nala. You're safe. Do you hear me? Maze and a few of your men brought you to your room."

Then he thrashed violently and in a split-second, brought up his knees. One of them hit her in the back and she fell on top of him, stretched across his upper body.

His eyes remained closed but he took a swing at her. His fist missed her head but some of his fingers caught in her hair. It *hurt*.

She shoved away from him and fell off the bed, landing on her ass. He thrashed more, made a pained sound, and she climbed to her feet, rushing to the panel.

"Maze!"

His voice came seconds later. "What's wrong, Nala?"

She glanced over her shoulder. Stag thrashed, turned, and almost rolled off the bed.

"Help!" She jerked her hand off the pad and ran back to him, almost tackling Stag to put him on his back and away from the side of the bed.

He fought and tried to buck her off. She shoved at his chest, attempting to pin him down, but he was incredibly strong.

"Stop! It's okay, Stag. You're going to hurt yourself."

85

Blood seeped through the bandage on his shoulder when she pressed her head to his chest to avoid a swinging arm directed her way. The bright red trailed toward her when he attempted to roll them into the wall, but she ignored it, keeping herself pressed tight against him, her arms around his waist.

Her gaze lifted to his face but his eyes remained closed. It was as if he wasn't awake enough to realize he wasn't still outside in his space suit, possibly having a flashback of fighting to survive.

She hoped Maze was close as the big cyborg under her rolled again and almost dumped them *both* off the bed. She braced one foot on the floor and shoved, pushing him back toward the center of the mattress.

* * * * *

They were going to kill him.

Stag fought against the three guards. They'd come to cause trouble, but he wasn't willing to let them put him inside one of the food-storage lockers to see how long it would take for his body to freeze. They were bored, and they'd targeted him for amusement.

One of them laughed. "Think it'll be okay when it defrosts?"

"They might have to replace the skin on the exterior if we leave it in there until the end of shift. It'll be an ice cube." He lunged at Stag, using a prodded weapon to try to stun him.

Stag twisted, avoiding it. "You'll be brought up on charges for this. Destruction of property is a criminal offense. I won't survive."

"*I?*" The one in charge laughed. "Look at it, trying to act like one of us. You're nothing but a skin droid. You're an *it*, and we want to see if you turn blue once that skin you're wearing starts to freeze over."

They didn't seem to care that it was against the law to injure him. Another one of the crew came at him, swinging a metal rod, aiming for his head.

Stag ducked, avoided the blow that would have knocked him out, and grabbed the rod. He tore it from the Earther's hand and swung it himself. All three jumped back.

"I thought you said it couldn't hurt any of us?" The youngest of the bunch backed up farther. "It looks pretty pissed."

The one who seemed to be in charge pulled his stunner weapon and pointed it at Stag. "You're programmed not to attack. Looks like it's defective to me. I say self-defense, what about you guys?"

Stag glared at the Earther. "Discharge that weapon and you'll set off alarms. Security will play the feeds to witness the event and they'll see that you came after me. I'm expensive." He glanced at the Earther's uniform and curled his lip. "You're *support staff*, not even military. They'll toss you out an airlock for the money you'll cost them to replace me. You and your two friends won't survive to see the end of your shift."

The Earther cursed and holstered his weapon. "Fuck you, skin droid! Get that thing. We'll hurt it where it doesn't show. No way am I letting this thing talk to me that way."

Stag tensed, shifting his grip on the rod, as the men spaced out around him. They wouldn't use weapons to set off the alarms, now that he'd reminded them of that safety feature. He couldn't kill them, but he wasn't about to allow them to cause him massive damage or death.

Two of them came at him. The fight was on.

* * * * *

Nala was grateful when Maze rushed into the room and came to help. He threw his body over Stag's lower half, grabbed his arms, and tried to pin them down.

"What happened?"

"Hell if I know! I changed his bandages and then he started fighting. I tried to keep him down. I didn't want him hitting his head if he fell off the bed or slammed into the wall."

"Move."

That wasn't an easy thing to do. She had to wiggle a bit to get off Stag and out from under part of Maze.

The door opened again as she climbed off the bed, and Hellion entered. "What's going on?"

"Get restraints," Maze ordered. "I need my med kit outside the door, too."

Hellion spun away but the door remained open. Nala stared at the corridor, tempted to flee.

It was a chance to escape—but where would she go? It was possible they had life pods on the ship. She had no idea the size of the vessel. Then again, if Stag had been telling her the truth, they were in the Pitch.

Stag yelled, the words not clear. She watched as Maze used more of his body to pin down the injured cyborg. Stag continued to fight whatever demons he saw in his sleep. She glanced at the door one last time, then rushed to the bed and gripped Stag's ankles when he tried to use his knees to kick at Maze, the way he'd done to her before.

"I should have paralyzed his limbs," Maze grunted.

It scared Nala that Stag wasn't waking. "What's wrong with him? Seizures?"

Stag jerked one of his legs out of her hold and nailed Maze in the back. She scooted to the side, waited for Stag to straighten his leg, then fell forward, using her entire body to hold them down. He still managed to lift her a few inches before dropping his legs back to the bed.

"I sedated him so he won't wake. Sometimes our bodies will react to dreams because of our dependency on our cybernetics."

"I thought you said they were down, drained, off...whatever." Stag lifted her again with his legs and she clutched at the other side of the mattress, trying to keep him from tossing her off completely.

"That's the problem."

Someone grabbed Nala from behind. One arm slipped around her chest, the other around her hips, and she was lifted off Stag. She would have fallen from the fast motion, once she was put on her feet, but Hellion almost hugged her, stabilizing her balance.

He flashed a smile. "Stay back, beautiful Nala. I have this. You could become bruised, and that would break my heart. I'd kiss them though."

Her mouth parted, astonished by the muscled cyborg, but Hellion turned away and grabbed one of Stag's ankles. He had dumped fabric restraints on the end of the bed and quickly fastened Stag's leg to the frame. He went to work quickly to restrain the other leg.

Nala backed up and watched as Maze and Hellion finished strapping Stag down. They tightened the restraints enough that he only had a few inches of movement. Maze had a rip in his sleeve, but otherwise looked okay. He opened the kit that Hellion must have carried in and yanked out an injector, programmed it, and pressed it against Stag's neck.

Stag stilled fast. Shouts still came out of him and he tossed his head, his expression pained, but he wasn't fighting anymore.

Maze turned and looked Nala over. "Did you sustain any damage?"

"I could check her over," Hellion offered.

She glanced at the cyborg, to find him smiling. "I'm good."

Maze cleared his throat. "Thank you, Hellion. You may go now. I have this under control."

Hellion stepped closer to Nala. "You really should let me take a look at you. I'd be happy to view every inch of your body to search for bruises."

"Hellion! Out. Now." Maze's tone deepened. "Flirt with her later."

"Fine." Hellion walked to the door but then stopped and turned. "Beautiful Nala? I would take orders from you. I'd do anything you asked." He licked his lips. "Often. As much as you wanted. Stag may have been offended when you believed we were sex bots, but it would be a privilege to be yours."

"Out!" Maze stepped between them.

The door sealed and Maze sighed, spun, and shook his head. "That one has emotional issues. I apologize."

She recovered. "He's, um, very friendly at least."

Maze moved to his kit and bent. "That's an interesting way to put it. He's juvenile, and at times downright annoying. It's no wonder the female ended their contract in record time."

"Can you say that in a way that makes sense?"

He closed the kit and rose, gripping it. "Marriage contract. A female cyborg accepted him into her family unit, but ended it within days. He doesn't do well in our society because of his flirtatious behavior. That's why he was assigned to Stag. He's got more patience than most others, and there are no females onboard."

"A player cyborg, huh?"

Maze cocked his head, peering at her. "Ah. It took me a moment to grasp the term. Hellion is impulsive, and allows his feelings to control most of his actions. He didn't flirt with other females when he was married, but she wasn't comfortable with his open affection toward her. It unnerved her. Cyborgs are more reserved. Hellion is not. It's considered a flaw."

She glanced at Stag. His lips were clamped together tightly. "What's going on with him? Is it a sign of brain damage?" That was her biggest fear.

"No. He's dreaming. It can happen at times when a cyborg is injured and partially sedated. I've paralyzed him from the neck down."

"Won't that make him stop breathing or something? It sounds horrible."

"No. He just can't move around now. It won't affect his organs. Can you tend to his shoulder?"

"He needs stitches."

Maze shook his head. "It will heal enough that they aren't required. We aren't like you. It's why we don't use them in such minor injuries. I must return to Control. Call me if there's another problem."

He started to leave, but paused. "He can still feel pain, so be aware of that."

"I'll be careful not to hurt him."

Maze left and she got the smaller med kit back on the bed, taking a seat next to Stag. He turned his head, muttered something, but seemed to calm a bit. She reached for the bandage on his shoulder. It was coated with blood near the bottom, which had been smeared over his skin. Maze probably would have to change his uniform. She figured it was probably bloody since he'd pressed Stag down with his body.

She got another wet cloth. Stag's skin was firm but remarkably warm and velvety soft. "It's just you and me again." She began to clean him. "I'd hate to know whatever was just going through your head."

It made her wonder just how bad a life he'd had while he'd been on Earth, if that was the cause of his nightmare. She paused, reached up, and caressed his cheek.

"Don't make me feel bad for you. You're starting to."

Chapter Seven

Nala came awake when she heard a low growl. She was curled into a ball between the wall and where Stag had been restrained on his back. Hellion and Maze had stretched him out, his arms and legs spread, so she'd had little space to sleep.

She lifted her head and found Stag's eyes open, the cyborg glaring at her.

"Do you know your name?"

"What have you done to me?"

She sat up, careful not to touch him. "What's your name? Do you remember?"

"I'll kill you, Nala."

He knew *hers*. That was a great sign. His distrust of her remained too. "Oh good. And I thought you might have suffered brain damage. You're still the same jerk. Woo-hoo."

"What have you done to me?"

She climbed over him, carefully trying to avoid touching him as best as she could. "I didn't put those restrains on you. Maze and Hellion did." She rolled her shoulders and turned, staring down at him. "You were injured. Do you remember what happened?"

His eyes closed then opened. "The decoy worked but debris hit me."

She wasn't sure what that meant. "You were outside in a space suit. I didn't get all the details except you had to be revived. You came back into the ship not breathing."

He clenched his jaw. "My neck was broken? Was my spine severed?"

It sank in, the reason why he'd ask. Compassion hit fast and hard. "No. It's just drugs. You're fine." She sat on the bed and put her hand on his chest. "See? Feel. It's just drugs. They're going to wear off and you can move everything once they do. The paralysis is temporary."

He arched his head a little, glancing at the restraints. "I thought *you* did this. Let me go."

"No 'I'm sorry for threatening to kill you', huh?"

He glowered at her.

"That's what I figured. Did you think I attacked you while you slept and broke your neck?" She snorted. "You really are paranoid. How do you think I'd get access to restraints like these? Do you keep them stashed inside your quarters? Are you kinky, Stag?"

"Take them off right now. That's an order."

She twisted a little and got more comfortable on the edge of the bed, amused. "Or what? You'll yell at me? What's it like being the one tied down?" She lifted her hand off his chest and then used one finger to press against him. "You're at the big bad Earther's mercy. What do you think I'll do?" She tapped him with her finger. "Kill you with my fingernail?"

"Take the restraints off, Nala."

94

She grinned. "You can't move anyway until those drugs wear off. Maze didn't say how long they'd last. Are you ticklish?" She trailed her finger over his ribs at his side, using four of them, lightening her touch.

He sucked in a sharp breath and she froze, surprised. Gooseflesh rose along his skin and his nipples beaded into tight nubs. She met his gaze.

He lifted his head, the only thing he could probably do. Fury showed in his eyes.

It amused her. "You are!"

"Don't touch me."

"I'm not a droid," she reminded him, enjoying it way too much that he was helpless. He deserved her torment a little after all he'd put her through. Karma was alive and well. "Ready to negotiate now, Stag? What are you willing to offer me if I don't tickle the hell out of you until Maze comes to check on his grumpy patient?"

"Stop touching me and remove the restraints. Don't make things worse for yourself, Nala."

That killed her good mood. "Oh, you mean like finding out that at some point, when I do get off this ship, it's only so I can be sold or whatever to some guy who will make me a sex slave? When were you going to drop that info on me?"

"You won't be a slave. You'll be assigned to a caretaker."

"Owner. Caretaker. Whatever you want to call it. Same difference. He'll still demand sex from me, right?"

95

He turned his head, seeming to concentrate on the door. She glanced at it, then him. "Are you trying to contact someone?"

He ignored her and closed his eyes. Frustration had him growling under his breath.

"Let me guess. Those electronics inside you can do that? The ones with a power drain right now?"

His eyes flew opened and he stared at her, looking surprised.

"Maze mentioned something about them having to recharge and it could take hours. Not working yet, huh?"

"Let me go, Nala."

"I'll take that as a no, they aren't. It's just you and me for a while."

"You'll pay for this."

"What am I doing?" She lightly raked her fingernails over his skin, not hurting him. "I'm only touching you."

"Stop."

"Is there something wrong with this? I mean, some jerk is going to put his hands on *me* at some point, and he won't care if I want him to or not. Why did you even bother to take me off the *Pride*? Do you get credits when you sell me? How much am I worth?"

"It's not like that."

"How is it?"

He pressed his lips together, making it clear he didn't plan to answer.

It pissed her off, and she sat up. He was probably afraid she'd kill him if he told her how much he was going to gain.

96

She faced him more fully, openly admiring his body. He had a great one, and his color was back to normal. He seemed fully recovered from what had happened, except for the drugs still in his system. He'd be able to link with his computer and call for help once his implants recharged. At least, she was pretty sure he could.

She reached out and pressed her hand on his chest, caressing him. "Does it bother you to be touched?"

"Stop."

"I'll take that as a yes." She leaned in, staring into his eyes. "You wanted to teach me what it's like if someone treated me like an android." She suddenly lifted up and straddled his body, bracing her legs on each side of his hips. "How about a little lesson for *you*?"

"What are you doing?"

She sat down so her ass rested on his pelvis and ran her hands over his chest, stroking from his shoulders down to his stomach. "Some asshole is going to touch me. I hopefully won't be restrained at the time, so maybe I'll be able to fight back, but you're cyborgs. I won't stand a chance of making him stop, will I? I know you're at least five times stronger than other guys. Minimum. They made you that way, right? My dad told me that. This is the future I get to deal with—thanks to you."

She suddenly leaned over and scooted down him a little more. His nipples were still erect. She opened her mouth and ran the tip of her tongue over one, then blew air across the puckered flesh.

It hardened even more, responding. Stag cursed.

She ignored him and pressed her lips around him, licked again, and then gently sucked. She used the lower edge of her teeth to lightly rake across the beaded tip of his nipple.

His breathing increased rapidly. She heard it...felt it since her face was pressed against his chest.

She released his nipple, glanced up, and found him glaring at her.

It made her smile as she went for the other nipple, giving it the same treatment.

The real surprise came when she felt him responding in *other* ways. Her pussy was pressed against his groin and his dick hardened. It wasn't something she could miss, since he'd been designed to be big in that area.

Nala released his nipple and lifted up a little, looking down their bodies. Stag was definitely hard. The small shorts revealed the bulge. She lowered her body down again and snuggly molded them together as she met his gaze.

"I bet that pisses you off. Considering I'm an Earther."

"It's just a basic physical reaction."

She laughed and sat up all the way. She tugged at her shirt, taking it off. His attention instantly fixed on her bared breasts. His cock twitched under her.

She placed the top next to her so she could grab it fast in case Maze returned. It would already be embarrassing to be caught tormenting Stag this way—but worth the risk to get a bit of revenge.

She reached up and cupped her breasts, massaging them. "How about if I play with myself, the way *you* did while I was lying next to you?"

He closed his eyes and turned his head. "I don't understand what you're trying to do beyond annoy me."

"Is that what you call it when you get hard? Don't watch then—but feel."

She lowered down again and latched onto one of his nipples with her mouth, sucking. She rocked her hips too, rubbing against his cock. He grew harder, and she had to admit he wasn't the only one having a physical reaction. It felt good to use the length of his shaft to stimulate her clit. Even with clothes between them, she grew wet fast, her pussy aching.

She lifted her head a little and stared at Stag. He kept his eyes closed but he'd bitten his lower lip, hard enough to turn it almost white. He'd probably cause himself to bleed if he didn't ease up, but she knew why he did it. He was trying to stay quiet. She released his nipple and he stopped torturing his lip.

She wiggled down his body and placed kisses over his ribs. "How pissed would you be if I got you off, Stag? Would that mess you up? An Earther doing that to you?"

"Stop touching me, Nala. I'll drop you off at any station you want and you can return to living with Earthers."

"I don't believe you. So much for cyborgs being honest."

She slid down him more, had to straddle one of his legs since they were slightly spread apart, and placed her hand over his cock, still trapped inside his shorts. The material was silky. She rubbed the rigid length with her palm, then her fingertips along the tip of it.

His cock jerked. He was big and rock hard. She watched his face.

He opened his eyes and lifted his head. The look he gave her showed desire and anger at the same time. "I'll make you regret this."

"Newsflash, Stag. I partially already do." She studied his body. "Why do you have to be so hot? Do us both a favor and just stop talking. You're the first man I've touched in over six years." She gripped the top of his shorts and tugged them down a few inches but they were trapped under his ass. "I might not have a choice later on of who I end up in bed with, but I do today. Tag—you're it."

It took both hands to wiggle his shorts down enough to free his cock. She lifted up, tapped the panel he kept his stuff in, and withdrew the bottle.

"What are you doing?"

She opened it and poured out lube. "You like to be touched. Like this?" She gripped him and gently squeezed, stroking his cock.

He threw his head back and hissed.

"Maybe like this?" She slowed the pace, sliding her hand low and avoiding the head, then stroking up and back down. "What feels better? My hand or yours?" She kept doing it, working him in that unhurried pace.

His stomach clenched, all the muscles bunching there. She froze. It had been a long time, but she still remembered some things.

"You're already about to come, aren't you?"

He lifted his head and the look in his eyes said it all. They were heavy-lidded and sultry. He looked like a man on the edge, and as if he'd kiss her if given the chance

She let go of his cock and crawled up him. He didn't say a word, but his gaze lowered to her breasts and he licked his lips.

He could bite her. It was a real fear. She put one hand on his shoulder, careful of the injured one, and pressed her breasts against his chest. She kept just enough distance between their mouths to jerk back if he lunged forward.

"You turn me on too. And I hate it. I guess we have that in common." She searched his eyes but she didn't spot any anger in them at that moment. "I'm even willing to admit this little lesson backfired on me because I'm wet. I haven't felt a man inside me in so long."

His gaze darted to her mouth, then back to her eyes.

She licked her lips. "Truce?"

"What do you want? You have me at a disadvantage." His voice came out really deep and husky.

Stag could be sinfully sexy when he wasn't being an ass.

"You mean because you're unable to move?"

"My implants are down. I can't deaden my responses."

"Physical ones?"

"Physical and emotional. Take off the restrains."

That was more honest than she'd expected him to be. She used her free hand and reached up, caressing his cheek. He pressed his face against

101

it instead of jerking away, seeking her touch. He wanted her too, and wasn't denying it.

"Can I kiss you or are you going to hurt me?"

He glanced at her mouth again. "Do it."

That wasn't an answer, but she was willing to risk it. She closed her eyes and moved in closer, touched his lips with hers, and licked the one he'd previously abused with his teeth. He opened up to her and she deepened the kiss. It had been ages, but it came back to her as he stroked her tongue with his.

He moaned, and she did too. He tasted like wine. The ache between her legs became worse and she rubbed against his stomach where she straddled him. He was so tall. Their bodies didn't line up right, and it frustrated her. She broke the kiss and found him watching her, passion easy to read in his blue eyes.

"I want you inside me. Yes?"

"Yes," he rasped.

She had to climb off him, and almost fell off the bed in her haste to remove her pants. None of her underwear had made the trip to his ship so it was just a matter of undoing the pants and shoving them down her legs. She grabbed the shirt though and put it back on.

"Why?"

She straddled him again, reached down between their bodies, and used the wetness to tease her own clit. "Anyone could just walk in. This will at least cover us a little if it happens."

He lowered his gaze, watching her hand move. "What are you doing?"

"You're close to coming." It felt good to rub the bundle of nerves. "Making sure you don't do it before I do."

"Let me see. Lift the shirt."

She sat up more, gripped the shirt and tugged it up to her stomach. Something brushed her ass and she twisted, seeing that Stag was still totally up to the task of being inside her. Her desire hiked more as she stroked her clit, the nub hardening, and she stared into his beautiful eyes.

"Ride me," he ordered.

"Close..." She was. She scooted back, keeping her finger moving over the swollen nub, and used her other hand to grip his cock. She spread her thighs a little more and rubbed the crown of his cock along the seam of her pussy.

Stag's breathing increased and she noticed his hands fist at the sides of the bed. Some of his motion was returning, the drugs wearing off. Time was running out before his implants would come back too, she figured. He'd be able to signal Maze to come, and then he'd be the one in control again.

She adjusted the angle of her hips, lined his shaft up with her entrance, and sank down on him slowly. She closed her eyes and stopped rubbing her clit. He was thick and her body resisted taking him. She bent forward, using his chest to brace herself as she pushed back against his lap, taking more of him.

It had been so long since she'd experienced that feeling of being filled, of having a man inside her. She moaned, rocked her hips, and took even more of him. He was huge and it felt incredible. He was so hard...

"Fuck," he hissed.

They were. She spread her fingers to brace better on his chest and started to rock back and forth. Moans tore from her throat and she didn't try to muffle them. She sank down on him all the way and just collapsed forward, laying on him as she rubbed their bodies together. It pressed her clit against his lower stomach. Each movement felt even better.

"Oh God! I'm going to come. It's been too long," she got out, frantically grinding against him now.

He thrust his hips upward suddenly, surprising her, but it felt so good as he took over, rocking them. It made her body slide against his. She clutched at his sides, just hanging on as they moved together. The climax tore through her with brutal force and she leaned forward, burying her mouth against his hot skin. He craned his neck, his jaw pressing against the top of her head.

He jerked, groaning, and she knew he was coming too.

He finally stopped bucking his hips under her and Nala panted, sprawled on top of him. She could feel her vaginal muscles still twitching in the aftermath around his cock buried inside her.

Long minutes passed. She didn't know what to say to him and was afraid to lift her head off his chest. He finally broke the silence.

"Take off my restraints, Nala."

104

He wasn't going to stop asking her to do that, obviously. It was time to face the consequences anyway. He didn't sound exactly angry but his tone implied he wasn't happy either. "You said yes," she reminded him.

"I did."

"What are you going to do to me?" She still wasn't willing to look at him.

"Do you want Maze or another member of my crew to find us this way? We need to use the cleansing unit and change the bedding, or they will guess we've had intercourse."

She flinched at the cold term. "You can move now, can't you?"

"I tried to break the restraints but couldn't. I didn't want you to know, hoping you'd take them off, thinking I was still helpless."

"How long?"

"It's been about five minutes since I regained the use of my limbs."

She lifted off him a little and raised her chin. He masked his expression as she studied him. "Implants?"

"Not yet, or I'd seal the door so no one could walk in. They could at any second."

"Are you going to hurt me?"

"I'd never abuse you."

That wasn't exactly what she wanted to hear. "What's your definition of that?"

"Release me. Don't make this worse."

"You mean by your crew finding out you had sex with an Earther?"

105

His lips pressed together in a grim line. "Nala, let me go."

She used his chest to straighten up. His cock remained hard inside her, apparent as since their bodies were still joined. She lifted up, separating them, and climbed toward the top of bed.

The restraints were easy to figure out. They were a two-pinch system on the back of his wrist. It took effort to squeeze hard enough for the lock to open, but it did, freeing one of his arms.

She almost expected him to grab for her throat but he twisted away, opening the other restraint himself. She ended up in the corner of the bed as he sat up and bent forward, reaching for his ankles.

He was flexible. She'd give him that. He got free and slid off the bed, yanking his shorts up his hips, but not before she got to glimpse a bit of his firm, rounded ass. It was a nice one. He turned then, his expression unreadable again.

"Use the cleansing unit. I'll change the bedding."

She was leery. "That's it? You're not going to get even?"

"I can't lock the door without my implants working. Get in the cleansing unit. Hurry. I'll use it next."

It seemed hiding the fact that they'd had sex was more important to him at that moment than getting revenge.

She crawled off the bed and dashed into the unit. He didn't try to stop her. She sealed the door, removed her shirt, and leaned against the wall. Stag would make her pay somehow. She had faith—and dreaded it.

Chapter Eight

Stag exited the cleansing unit in his uniform. He had already changed the bedding before using it, and he refused to even look at Nala. He was aware of her sitting on the bed. She'd put on another outfit since he'd tossed her pants down the laundry chute. They had evidence on them of her becoming aroused.

He strode across the room and laid his palm on the sensor. Nothing happened. It pissed him off and unnerved him. The door had been locked and he couldn't link to open it. Anger came next. He was effectively locked inside his own quarters. The computer wasn't registering him as a crew member.

"Do you want out?"

Her voice was close to him. He jerked his hand off the panel and spun. She had left the bed and now stared up him from just feet away. "Isn't Maze checking on my progress? It's his job."

She inched around him and touched the pad. "Maze?"

A click sounded, then the medic's voice came from the com speaker. "What is wrong, Nala?"

She sighed. "Your patient is up and wants out. The doors won't open."

"I'm on my way."

She released the pad and faced him. "He set that up so I could get ahold of him if you had any problems."

That pissed him off. "I plan to have words with him."

"Because he left you in my care?"

"Yes." He wouldn't deny it.

"Well, it sounded like shit hit the fan. I don't know the details since I'm *persona non grata* onboard. It was a good thing he didn't dump you in some room alone, since I was here when you started thrashing around."

"Explain."

"You were out, but your body wasn't. It looked like you were fighting someone and almost threw yourself out of the bed. I had to kind of tackle you to keep you down until help arrived. It's why you were immobilized. You might have bashed your head open or something."

"You're saying you saved my life?" He shook his head. "I don't believe it."

"Not your life. Just kept you from being injured more than you already were."

"Are you trying to make me feel indebted to you? That event never happened."

"You're such an ass." She spun, lifted her shirt, and yanked it up. "This is from your knee. I managed to dodge your fists."

Dismay hit him at the huge bruise covering her skin. It was about a four inch diameter mark—and could definitely be from a knee. The discoloration looked painful, and it looked as if she'd taken quite a blow.

She dropped her shirt and spun. "But wait—I'm just making that up. Fuck you." She stormed around him and sat on the bed. "Mental note made. Next time I'll let you slam into the floor. It might knock some sense into you."

The door opened and Maze came in. "Stag. How do you feel?"

"Get your med kit and check Nala. She has damage to her back."

"I'm fine. It's just a bruise."

Maze walked closer to her and knelt by the bed where she sat. "Why didn't you say something? You didn't mention you were hurt when we stabilized Stag. Is that when it happened?"

"According to him," she jerked her head at Stag, "that never happened, so no. I must have kneed *myself* in the back. Apparently, I'm super flexible like that."

That angered Stag further. "Treat her. I'll be in Control."

He left fast before he said something he'd regret. Nala had a way of making a fool out of him, making him feel like the ass she kept claiming he was.

The lift opened for him since it was motion-sensor controlled. He entered Control seconds later. "Status?"

Veller rose from his command seat, stepping aside. "It's good to see you recovered."

"Take the chair. I am here to get an update."

Veller frowned.

"I'm offline. I can't link to our ship. You can. The hull patch?"

"Complete. No additional damage. You almost had it melded on when the incident occurred."

He didn't want to think about when his suit had been pierced. It had been traumatic. He'd survived, and that was all that mattered. "Any other problems?"

"None. We're just watching the countdown until we try to leave the dead zone."

"Display it for me."

Veller sat back down and placed his hand on the pad at the chair. Stag wished he could do that. The front monitor came on and showed how much time remained.

"We've seen no other signs of thrusters. No other bombs attached except to the one solar panel that blew."

"Good."

"We're in a safe sector until we move. They would have been drawn to our hull if any were within range. We kept an eye on the unaffected solar panels as they drifted outward, until we lost visuals on them. They remained intact."

"You didn't use exterior lights to track the panels, did you?"

Veller shook his head. "No light sources. I remembered your orders. Were your implants damaged?"

"I can't be certain until they are online again."

"That must be difficult."

He met Veller's direct stare. "It is."

"I imagine it would be like losing a limb. Is it?"

Stag's patience came to an end. "Why your curiosity?"

Veller slid his gaze away. "I apologize."

Stag was tempted to return to his quarters and avoid the rest of the crew until he was back to standard, but that would mean spending time with Nala. He took a seat at coms. "Crew status?"

"Hellion and Parqel are doing routine maintenance. Kelis and Yammer just went off shift and are sleeping. Maze is currently in your quarters."

"Two men should always be in Control at all times. You know the rules."

"Maze was called away by the Earther. You're here now."

But I'm useless. Stag refused to share that information. "Get Maze back here."

"Contacting him now." He paused. "He's on his way."

Stag fisted his hands in his lap and looked at the dark space being displayed on the pads. He could watch for lights. He didn't need his cybernetics for that.

Maze returned for shift duty within minutes. He took a seat at the weapons station and glanced at Stag. "Would you allow me to scan you?"

"I'm fine. How long will I be offline?"

"Your systems should reboot soon."

"Why did this happen?" He was furious that he couldn't access parts of himself. He kept trying but they didn't respond.

"You suffered heart failure. It was better to shut everything down than risk parts being damaged by the electrical current it took to bring you back."

"Understood."

"Nala refused to allow me to scan her. I did insist on looking at the injury."

He didn't like the medic seeing Nala without her shirt. "Conclusion?" He hated that he'd hurt her, even if he hadn't been aware of doing it. There was no honor in harming someone so weak. She was little and fragile.

"It will heal. She said she had no pain from moving her arms or taking deep breaths. It's doubtful any bones were broken. It's just soft tissue damage. I'd still like to scan her."

"Leave her alone for now." Stag just wished he could stop thinking about her. An image flashed inside his mind of her head bent, her mouth suckling at his nipple. He'd never experienced anything like it—or what happened after.

His cock began to respond and he shifted in the chair, focusing on the pad. It had to be because he'd been vulnerable without his implants. He couldn't mute any of his responses to her. "Right now we have more important things to deal with."

He'd avoid Nala until he was completely in control of his emotions and physical responses again, and forget all about what had happened on his bed. That was the best course of action to take. He'd nearly died, after all, and had woken disorientated. That had to be why he'd allowed her to get to him.

No Earther would get the best of him. They were deceitful, and males who fell under their seduction were naïve. Stag wasn't.

* * * * *

Nala woke when the door opened and Stag entered. He didn't spare her a glance as he began to remove his boots. He stored them in one of the touch drawers that slid back into the wall when he was done. He entered the cleansing unit next.

"So we're ignoring each other?" She sighed, lay back down, but scooted to the wall to make room for him when the cleansing unit went off. She drifted back to sleep until he spoke.

"Did you eat?"

She rolled over, opening her eyes. He'd dimmed the lights and only wore a pair of shorts. Memories of him without them surfaced, but she tried to wipe that from her mind. "Yes. Maze not only brought me dinner but gave me a shot to help speed up healing."

"How is your back?"

"Fine. How was your shift?"

He turned away, crossed the room and stretched his arm up. She knew that drawer—and it pissed her off as he opened it and withdrew the belts.

"No way. Nope."

He gazed back at her. "What?"

"You're not restraining me so you can sleep. Give me a break."

"It's a requirement."

"Fuck you." She rolled onto her side, back to him, and curled her arms to her chest. "I could have killed you when you were helpless. I didn't. You should seek treatment for your paranoia, if cyborgs have therapists. You're a mental case, Stag."

The bed dipped. "Give me your wrists."

She curled into a tighter ball. "I should have smothered you with your pillow when I had the chance."

"Nala," he warned. "Wrists. Now."

She was tempted to flip him off but he had fast reflexes. He might grab her hand if she exposed it to him. "Good night. I'm going back to sleep now."

"Don't make me force you."

She turned a little more, pulling her arms inside her shirt and pressing them against her skin. "Sleeping now. Go somewhere else if you can't trust me."

"You're acting childish."

"And you're acting like an unreasonable ass."

He surprised her when he gripped her waist and rolled her flat onto her back, straddling her in a heartbeat. He sat on her hips with his spread thighs pinning her in place, but kept most of his weight off. She glared up at him as he noticed what she'd done. Her arms were still curled tight to her chest, under her shirt. He frowned.

"Stop being a control freak. Get off me."

"Wrists." He had the restraints thrown over his bare shoulder, the other one still bandaged.

"No."

He gripped the lower edge of her shirt and tugged it up a little, revealing inches of her stomach. He paused, staring at it. "Wrists," he rasped. "Or I'll be forced to find them myself."

"Let me help you with that." He was going to win in a physical contest. She lifted her shirt, shoving it up and over her head, then crossed her arms again, curling her hands between her breasts. "There."

He stared at her chest. Her breasts were pushed up by her arms, exposed. A muscle flexed near his mouth but he didn't move.

"Just grab them. Go ahead."

He held very still.

"My wrists...to be clear."

His gaze lifted and he reached for the restraints. She tensed. He was going to force her arms up and tie her to the top of the bunk again. It would cost him though, since she'd be sleeping topless next to him.

He tossed the belts at the head of the bed and bent, his fists catching his weight on each side of her near her shoulders as he crouched down. He leaned in, holding her gaze. "What are you doing?"

"I'm not suffering alone."

"What does that mean?"

She slowly reached up and slid her fingers into his hair, stroking the short strands. He had thick, great hair. "You want me tied up next to you? Fine. But it's going to bother you that I'm topless. So do it." She released his hair and lifted both arms up, arching her back. It was provocative and she knew it. "If I remember right, being tied up and naked saved my life. You must have a fondness for seeing me that way. Want the pants too? Take them."

He didn't move but he wasn't holding her gaze anymore, instead watching her breasts.

"You're attempting to seduce me to see if you can."

"I already did," she boasted. "You might want to pretend nothing happened, but it did. It felt really good too."

He lifted one hand and reached for the belt. She tensed. He might want to strangle her with it for the taunt she'd just thrown down, but she didn't think he'd really hurt her. He would have by now if he really hated her. She was starting to suspect that was a problem for him.

"You go too far, Nala. It's as though you enjoy angering me."

"It beats you being so cold." She reached for him and splayed her hand on his chest. "Warm up, Stag. I like you when you're hot." She brushed her thumb over his nipple and it hardened, turning instantly erect.

He climbed off her—and she knew she'd pushed him too far.

Stag gently wrapped his fingers around her wrist and secured it with the belt, then attached the other end to the frame above her. She offered

116

up the other one without making him fight for it. He said he was a person but he could be as cold as a machine. She'd tried to reach him, but he wasn't going to let his guard down twice. He didn't say it, but she understood.

"I'll explain a part of cyborg society to you."

She held still as he attached her other wrist. "Fantastic."

He sat on the edge of the bed and put his back to her. "We have family units. They are the same as an Earther marriage…only your kind murdered most of our women. So few survived that we had to adjust the concept. Women take on more than just one husband, so most of our men have the opportunity to be a part of a family." He turned then, watching her. "Our women are very selective of the men they choose to share homes with. They have various methods of judging prospective men. One is their job title and status. Another is their genetics. Flaws are not permitted."

"Like being paranoid? Do you have a wife?" She hated the idea, already jealous, and even a bit horrified, because what if he wasn't single? They'd had sex. His wife had other husbands, if what he said was true, so maybe cheating was accepted as the norm with cyborgs. It still didn't sit right with her.

"I'm single. When I was younger, I considered joining into a family unit until I became aware of the ramifications."

"What would those be?"

"The wives control every aspect of their husbands' lives. They aren't allowed to make a decision without consulting her first and getting her agreement."

"Ah. Control freak you said hell no to that." He wasn't married and wouldn't ever be. She was relieved by that news.

"Some of the women had certain other requirements, if you passed the status and genetic ones." He stood up, walked to the end of the bed, and leaned over. "Physical ones."

He gripped the bottom of her sleeping pants and tugged hard. He ripped them down her legs and she gasped, stunned. He tossed them aside as he straightened up and hooked his thumbs into the waist of his shorts, easing them lower.

"You want to play at seduction, Nala? You're out of your league." He freed his cock, already semi-hard, and shoved his shorts low enough to let gravity take them to the floor before stepping out of them. "I'm the best at everything I decide to do, so I've studied everything about a woman's body." His gaze languidly trailed over her body. "Cunnilingus. Stamina. Prepare to be schooled, little Earther."

She was staggered by the change in him. He climbed on the bed, gripped her ankles, and lifted them to place her feet on his chest. He lowered to sit on his legs on the bed, skimmed his hands down the underside of her calves to her knees, then shoved them wide apart. He dropped forward, going flat on his stomach. It put his head right over her pussy. He kept watching her, licked his lips and smiled.

118

She would even call that spark she saw in his gorgeous blue eyes malicious.

"You want hot? You're going to get it. I'm going to set you on fire, Nala. You're going to beg me to fuck you, and I'm going to. Do you know why?"

No one had ever spoken to her that way before, and the things he threatened to do sounded heavenly. She didn't care what his motives were. "Don't be a dick."

His eyes narrowed; she was pretty sure that response pissed him off. "No words then. Just learn."

He shoved her thighs farther apart, his strong hands clutching them to adjust her pussy the way he wanted, then he dipped his head.

She thought he might tease her, but she was wrong. He licked her clit, teased it, and then clamped his mouth around that bundle of nerves with a near roughness that had her almost flinching.

The one boyfriend she'd had was super gentle when he'd gone down on her, but it seemed Stag didn't know the meaning of the word as he began to suck and lash his tongue against her clit.

She twisted her wrists, grabbed hold of the belts and squeezed her eyes closed. Pleasure and ecstasy radiated through her until it was almost painful. She was going to come hard and fast. Moans tore through her and her body grew rigid, every muscle locking up in anticipation of him getting her off. He didn't disappoint, sending her over the edge. She cried out as her hips bucked, the climax brutal.

He didn't stop. She fought to get air into her lungs and frantically struggled to break away from his mouth, because she was oversensitive, but he stayed locked on her, licking and sucking.

Words came out of her mouth as she thrashed on the bed but he easily held her down. It was pain and pleasure. She lost track of time, couldn't think, and was shocked when another burst of rapture tore through her.

He eased off her clit then and she lay panting, her body coated in sweat.

"I'm just starting, Nala." His voice came out deeper. He released one of her thighs and she moaned when he ran his fingers down the seam of her pussy. "So wet. So ready for this."

She cried out when he pushed two fingers inside and began to fuck her with them. He curved his fingers a little and quickened the pace. She tried to close her legs because it felt too intense, too good, but he pushed his shoulder against her free leg to pin it to the bed and lowered his mouth, trapping her clit with his lips. He unleashed his tongue again.

The cyborg was going to kill her. She came a third time, and would have screamed, except she didn't have the strength or will. Her moans had left her throat feeling a bit raw. He pulled his mouth away as she rode out the climax, her vaginal muscles squeezing around his fingers. He slowly moved them, drawing out the orgasm.

He withdrew his fingers finally and released her thigh with his hand, lifting his shoulder off her other one.

Nala opened her eyes, out of breath, and stared at him as he climbed over her leg and stretched out on his side next to her.

"Now I'm going to fuck you."

He grabbed her hip and turned her onto her side, facing the wall. He was so strong. She'd give him that. While she felt like a wet noodle that had been wrung out. He hooked her around the waist, pressed up against her back, and then let his hand skim over her stomach to her hip, then over the top of her thigh. He slid his hand farther, grasping and lifting her leg. He scooted down, molding his lower stomach against the curve of her ass as he hiked her leg a little higher.

"Lift your head."

It took effort but she did it. He slid his other arm under her cheek, his biceps becoming her pillow. They were plastered together spoon style. He curled his knees, shoving her bottom leg forward on the bed. His stiff shaft ended up wedged against her pussy when he adjusted them one more time. He let the hand holding her leg trail lower, just under her knee, and hooked it over his thigh. He let go, reached over her hip, and gripped his cock.

He slid the head of it against her pussy and she moaned as he entered her, curving his body even tighter around hers, until he was seated deep.

He twisted the arm under her head a tiny bit to jerk her even closer to his chest. "Your smaller size is an advantage right now. You're trapped inside my arms."

She actually liked it. He was wrapped around her tight, and he was so warm. She just wanted to pass out and sleep like that. She even yawned, completely spent.

His mouth moved next to her ear and he chuckled. "Worn out so easily? You're in bed with a cyborg, Nala."

He arched his back. She could feel his stomach press tighter against her ass. It also withdrew him a bit from inside her, his cock moving. He thrust his hips, driving back into her deep. She moaned and tugged at the restraints holding her arms above her head. One was pinned under *his* arm though, so she couldn't move that one. The belts didn't have much give in them this time.

"We covered cunnilingus but we haven't gotten to stamina yet. I can do this to you for hours."

He moved, slowly fucking her. It felt incredible. Nala moaned, and Stag cupped her stomach, ran his hand lower, his fingers pressing up against her clit. Every glide of his hips had him massaging her intimately.

"Don't touch me there," she pleaded. "Too sensitive."

"You don't know the meaning of the word yet." He nuzzled his face against her throat and began to place kisses on her shoulder. He thrust into her deeper, faster, and applied more pressure against her clit.

Nala cried out, unable to form words anymore.

Stag *was* going to kill her. It just wasn't in a way she'd ever imagined. He was going to screw her to death—and probably give her a heart attack brought on by orgasms.

Stag used Nala's shoulder to muffle the sounds he made as his semen emptied into her pussy. His entire body quivered from the strength of the release. He'd had to use his implants a few times to deaden the feel of her. She sheathed his dick too well and he would have ejaculated too fast otherwise.

He'd brought her to release three more times since he'd put her on his lap. The third time, he'd known she couldn't take any more. Her body had been trembling too much. He'd let go of his control at that point, finishing them both off for the evening.

"Do you want me to make you come again, Nala?"

"Can't," she weakly mumbled.

He smiled. "Was that hot enough for you?"

She didn't answer, and he realized she'd already fallen asleep. He gently reached down, adjusted her leg he'd kept pinned over his, and laid it over her other one. He withdrew his dick from her body and reached up, using one hand to untie her wrists. She'd sleep for hours without waking. He'd worn her out.

He connected with the computer, adjusting the temperature again. He'd cooled the room while they'd been having sex but now he raised it so she wouldn't get cold.

He need to move her head off his arm but hesitated to do so. He shifted his body just enough to snag his pillow, draw it closer and shove it under his head. He carefully put his other arm around Nala, dragging her close. It took one more adjustment to drag her pinned arm down so he wasn't resting on it anymore.

It would be logical if he continued to keep her tucked against him. He'd wake if she tried to get free of his arms, alerting him to any danger she may pose. He gazed down at her. She wasn't big or strong enough to hurt him, as an Earther. Not without a weapon.

She lowered her arm in her sleep and tucked it near her chest, but her fingers curled around his wrist. The weight of them felt nice. Everything about having her this close, their skin pressed together, was pleasant. He imagined ending his shift and coming to his quarters to repeat what they'd done on a daily basis.

The knowledge also came that Nala had thoroughly corrupted him. Earthers were not to be trusted, but he had already considered keeping her. He wanted to roll away...but he just couldn't do it. He wanted to hold her for a little bit longer.

It would be the last time. In the morning, he'd do whatever it took to shut down the attraction he felt toward her. He was Stag. Not some foolish lovesick cyborg with a death wish.

Nala was a distraction he didn't need. The crew was at risk. The Markus Models wanted to create conflict with Earth. He and his crew were routinely sent on the most dangerous missions. It was why he only accepted single men with no family units on his shuttle. She needed to be transferred off the *Varnish*.

It was settled. He'd get them out of the dead zone, then fly straight to Garden. She'd be out of sight, and would no longer be a temptation.

124

Chapter Nine

Stag noted the way Nala moved after she'd exited the cleansing unit and took a seat on the bed. "Tender?"

She seemed surprised at his question when she looked up. "I thought you weren't talking to me. You showered, dressed, and just pointed for me to do the same."

"Answer me."

"A little."

He might have been too rough with her. "Do you need a medic? Are you hurt?"

"You're big. I think a few muscles got pulled last night. It's not exactly like I'm used to having sex, especially that much of it at once. But I'm fine."

"Any bleeding?" The thought bothered him. She was an Earther. And a small one, at that. He should have been more aware of her frailties.

"No."

"Did you check?"

"I'm fine, Stag. Stop, or I'll think you care about me. You wouldn't want that."

"I'll have food brought to you. I need to go on shift. Today, we're leaving the dead zone."

She stood. "What are our chances of actually getting out?"

"Good."

"Is that the truth?"

"I don't lie."

Her eyebrows arched, as if she didn't believe him.

"You're on a ship with cyborgs. We're careful with our calculations."

"You're saying you're smarter than all the other people who have been lost out here, right?"

"Yes."

"I'll buy that. Will you com me and let me know how it goes?"

"I'll return when my shift is over." He spun toward the door. It opened but Nala grabbed his wrist with both of her hands. He halted and turned, staring at her. "What?"

"Can I go with you?"

"No."

"Your hours are always different. You could be gone a really long time. I don't want to just pace around your room and worry. Please?"

"No."

"Have a heart. Actually, I know you have one. I've heard it beat. There's nothing to do in here. You don't have books, no entertainment system, nothing. You say you don't want to be cruel to me, so allow me to go with you. I'll be on my best behavior. I'll worry and go nuts just pacing in here."

He stepped away from the door, pushing up against her, and it closed them inside. "Why would you worry whether we get out of the dead zone or not, when you're confined to my quarters either way?"

"I'm going crazy in here. Ever hear of confinement sickness? I spent a lot of time in my quarters on the *Pride* but I had things to occupy my time. I know you don't want anyone to know we've done more than just sleep together on your bed. Is that it? I could have told Maze, but I haven't. And I won't. Your secret is safe. Please let me go with you."

"For what purpose?"

"There are three hundred and twenty-six tiles on your ceiling. I know. I've counted them more than once. I can tell you how many drawers I've found that aren't clearly defined. I've touched every part of the walls where I could reach. Not to snoop through your stuff, since most of them are locked, but because I had nothing else to do. I'm going crazy, Stag. Please? I just want out of this room. I'd rather watch paint dry than stay in here for another day. At least the color of it changes in slight variations after hours."

"You would be a distraction I can't allow if I took you to Control with me."

"I won't say a word. I'll be quiet. Shove me in a corner and I'll sit on the floor." She released his wrist with one hand and placed it over his chest. "I'll do whatever you say. No argument. You give me an order and I'll do it. Done."

He peered into her eyes and his thoughts instantly went to a sexual request. His lips parted but he refused to say it.

127

"Tell me to jump, I'll jump. Want me to stand on my head? I'll do it. Just please don't leave me in here."

Blood rushed to his dick and desire ignited. It was a once-in-a-lifetime opportunity, and he couldn't resist. "Would you drop to your knees and open my pants?"

He'd surprised her. Her eyes widened but then her cheeks turned a little pink. "I'll blow you if you let me tag along with you today. I owe you for last night. I'm not as expert at oral sex as you are, but I know the basics."

Stag instantly killed his emotions instead, shutting down his physical arousal with his implants when a hail came through. It was a buzz in his head that let him know one of his crew was politely attempting to reach him. He tore his gaze away from her and reached out, pressing his hand on the pad to open coms.

Kelis spoke. "We've got our solution and are ready for you to evaluate it."

"I'll be right there." He cut coms by lifting his palm off the pad, and then looked at Nala again. "You may go with conditions. Are you ready to hear them?"

"You have my full attention."

"You do not speak or move around. It will distract my crew."

"Done."

His gaze lowered to her mouth. She had a soft, sweet one. He couldn't wait to discover what it would feel like when she gave him oral sex.

128

It was a bad decision, taking her with him to Control, but he wasn't going to pass up the payment. Cyborg women didn't give oral sex, and the sex bots on stations had felt nice but they weren't sentient. They had been programmed with motion patterns that he detected while he'd made use of them. Nala would be a unique experience.

It was easier to think of it that way, as opposed to the fact that he just wanted her to touch him again.

"You do everything I say without argument or hesitation."

"I swear."

He placed his hand over hers on his chest, trapping it there. "When we're off shift later, I get to evaluate your skill level of performing oral sex."

Pink fused into her cheeks again but she didn't hesitate to nod. "It's a promise."

"The crew is not to know we've had intercourse. Don't speak to them."

"I understand. Does it embarrass you?"

He couldn't miss the way her mouth tightened, almost into a frown.

"I'm their commander. It's my job to avoid discord amongst my crew."

"You think they would get upset that we had sex because cyborgs distrust anyone from Earth? Maybe think you were some kind of traitor?"

"They might want equal access to your body."

She paled and her body stiffened.

He felt guilty, identifying her fear. That scenario was possible but he mostly didn't want to deal with their comments. His crew tended to express their thoughts. "It's best if they don't know."

"I won't say a word."

"Let's go. You stay at my side and do as I say. You break your word, and I'll have you escorted immediately back to my quarters. Clear?"

"Yes. Thank you."

He released her hand and shrugged her other one off his wrist. "No touching."

She backed up. "I'll glare at you a lot. How is that?"

He wasn't certain if she was trying to make a joke or if he'd angered her for real. "That's fine. Let's go." He opened the door and allowed her to follow him to the lift. She'd get a better idea of what kind of shuttle class the *Varnish* was, but it wasn't as if she was a security risk. She'd be taken to Garden, not to an Earther station, where she could report everything she'd learned about cyborgs to their authorities.

They made a quick stop and he got her some power bars and water. He led her into Control after she downed them and pointed to a seat in the corner. "Sit there."

She spun, walked to it, and seated herself. He noted Kelis, Parqel, and Hellion appeared astonished by her presence. Stag took his own seat and laid his hand on the pad, reading the information they'd assembled for him, double checking their calculations.

"Hello, Nala." Hellion broke the silence. "You look lovely today."

"Silence," Stag ordered. "She's not here. Ignore her."

Hellion frowned at him. "But she is."

He shot him an infuriated look. "I decided she'd be safer here than in my quarters. This area is more protected if we suffer massive damage. Now face forward and pay attention to your station. Today is not a day to become distracted. Am I clear?"

Hellion nodded, turning in his chair. "Of course. Don't say it. I know. Turn off my emotions."

Stag sighed. "We need to be at our best." He had the countdown show on the main screen. "We'd all like to see home again. Do not forget our number-one priority on every mission we take."

"Agreed," Kelis stated.

"Protect our people," Hellion grunted. "Against those skin droids, in this case."

Parqel spoke softer. "I always expected to die, but not like this, trapped in dead space. We're getting out of here. I swore I'd be taken out during battle."

"You might get your wish," Stag reminded him. He placed his hand on the pad again, calling the rest of his crew to Control. They came, expecting the order.

Yammer and Veller had two large bags each slung over their shoulders and took positions at the back of the room, near the doors. They touched the emergency panels and buckled themselves against the bulkheads, standing. Stag noticed the confusion on Nala's face.

"They aren't here for you," he informed her. "We're going to leave the dead zone. I have faith in our skills." He said that to all of his crew. "The Markus Models could be out there waiting for us the moment we exit. Every weapon aboard our ship is here for us to use if we're boarded."

The doors opened and Maze entered, two large kits in hand. He nodded at Stag and took one of the chairs, securing his medical equipment against his console so they wouldn't move if they took heavy damage or lost gravity.

Stag faced the front screen. "Buckle in tight." He noticed Maze had followed his directive, two weapons strapped to his thighs. He held the medic's gaze. "You know your orders."

Maze jerked his head in the affirmative, grim.

"Don't shoot me twice," Hellion muttered. "Make the first one count if you have to kill us to avoid capture."

"I promise," Maze swore.

Stag didn't envy the medic's position at that moment. He was supposed to save lives, not be ordered to take them if they were going to be captured. "We must protect Garden at all costs."

Nala swallowed hard and tightened the belts that strapped her to the seat. She had followed the conversation—and wished she hadn't. The cyborgs weren't next to the doors to keep her from escaping. They were there to protect Control if those skin droids that had murdered her crew managed to dock with Stag's ship. And Maze was under orders to kill them all if he was left with no other choice.

132

As a captain, she understood. She'd given her crew the same order if they'd ever been boarded by pirates and all hope was lost. Nala had decided a fast death at the hand of one of her crew would be more merciful than being raped and held captive to birth a mutant. All reports stated most captured women died during childbirth, but some lingered for months after, dying agonizing deaths from radiation poisoning.

Stag's reason for giving that order was different. Cyborgs had information that would put their home planet's location at risk. It was Stag's job to make certain that never happened.

They had a countdown showing on the main screen at the front of the small room, though their Control was bigger than the one on her ship. She watched the time pass, keeping her word to be silent. The cyborgs spoke in hushed tones, checking systems and preparing for whatever they were going to do.

The Cyborgs were very different from her crew. Her men would have been filled with nervous chatter, sharing raunchy jokes to break tensions, and lots of cursing would have gone down if they believed an attack was imminent.

Part of her was filled with awe. Stag's calm attitude set the tone for his crew. He was a great captain. Her respect for him grew.

"Prepare," Stag finally stated. "We don't know what will await us out there but I have faith in every single one of you. Be aware of the systems under your control. They will attempt to hack us, and they have a habit of targeting nonessential systems. Are you ready?"

The mood changed in the room and Nala could sense it. It wasn't fear but more of a determination. Every cyborg was prepared to die defending each other and the ship. Maze would only take their lives if they were overrun by those flesh bots.

A shiver ran down her spine, wondering if he was under orders to shoot her too.

She hoped so. Those things probably wouldn't tie her to a bed to use as bait a second time. Stag had told her they'd killed one of her men by dissecting him while he was still alive. Being shot sounded kind in comparison.

She gripped her belts as the engines came online, the vibrations growing stronger.

"On zero." Stag paused. "Be prepared for some jarring. Our stabilizers will experience a slight delay."

Hellion spoke. "They weren't designed for this."

"No, they weren't," Stag agreed. "The *Varnish* is tough though. We've keep it in excellent condition." He paused. "Mark. Three. Two. One."

In the next instant, Nala was thrown back against her seat. The floor under her and the chair shook, and she realized what they'd done. Stag had powered up the engines and they'd gone from a dead stop to a full burn. That maneuver would have been impossible on the *Pride*. Her older transport would have incurred massive damage.

The stabilizers kicked in and everything stopped shaking, restored enough so she didn't feel the forward motion.

"One solar panel broke loose but it's nonessential," Kelis stated. "No other damage registering."

"Keep monitoring," Stag ordered. He began to count down again from nine.

Nala wondered what they were going to do next. She kept quiet though, knowing their lives depended on getting out of the Pitch. They'd eventually run out of food, water, or the ship's systems would begin to break down if they remained inside, unable to ever dock somewhere.

"Brace," Stag warned, instead of saying zero when he reached it.

The belts dug into her hard, her body thrown forward as he reversed thrusters. She watched on the monitor as their course changed, Stag turning the ship. It began to shake and rattle, the stabilizers and gravity having difficulty compensating for the violent changes in speeds. Neither went out completely but she could feel the roll. It made her stomach queasy.

A loose item, the size of her hand, slid across the floor, then up the wall, and she knew it wasn't her imagination. The entire ship was in a sideways spin.

"Now," Stag rasped.

She was thrown back against her seat again and the item came sliding along the floor toward her feet. She identified it as some kind of pad attachment, a metal clipping device. She lifted her feet and it missed hitting her toes.

The cyborgs were crazy. They'd taken off fast, came to a complete stop, and were now full burning again.

She closed her eyes, braced her feet, and clung to her belts. The pressure of her body being shoved into the seat eased, and she dared watch what was going on again.

"Eight seconds," Kelis stated. He began to count down.

Nothing happened when he stopped the countdown, and Stag actually cursed.

"What?" That burst out of her mouth.

He didn't answer her. Hellion did. "We should be out of the dead zone but we're not."

It was a nightmare. They were trapped in the Pitch.

"Hold course." Stag sounded too calm. "Maintaining speed."

Blackness filled the screen—but then she spotted a light.

"There!" She pointed, forgetting her promise to Stag in her excitement.

"We see it." He turned his head and shot her a dirty look. "Quiet, Nala."

She sealed her lips. The belts dug into her as the ship reversed thrusters. Stag had to be doing everything by drastic measures for the stabilizers to be that out of sync. Nala was tempted to ask him why. The captain part of her protested his methods. He could have slowed their speed gradually, causing less stress on the ship.

More lights appeared in the distance. They were seeing stars.

The cyborg crew had actually done it. They'd found their way out of the Pitch.

It was the first time anyone who'd ever entered it had escaped, to her knowledge.

"Sensors are limited." Kelis sounded tense. "I'm not picking up anything but they aren't reliable at this distance."

"I'm easing us out slow and releasing some oxygen." Stag lowered his voice to almost a whisper. "We don't want to show on their sensors."

Frustration burst through her. That made no sense! *Every* ship could be detected on sensors, except those fancy ones some of the military had made. She couldn't hold her thoughts any longer.

"What are you talking about? Venting oxygen? Why?"

Stag didn't turn that time in his seat. He ignored her.

Veller was closest to her by the exit doors. He cleared his throat and whispered, "The Genesis Four shuttles are completely reliant on sensors to fly. We have someone who is familiar with their design and their weaknesses. We'll read as a chunk of debris or an asteroid to them if we move slow. Venting oxygen creates a mass around our ship that confuses the sensors when they try to read the shapes they're picking up."

She understood—and it was brilliant. "Thanks."

He inclined his head. Her next concern was how much oxygen they had to vent out, and if life support could sustain all of them. She didn't ask though. Avoiding capture and attack was paramount at the moment. She probably would have made the same choice if she'd known it could have saved her crew. All human ships kept emergency tanks of oxygen, and she hoped the cyborg ships did, too. It would be tough being attached to a breathing rig for days until they could reach a station, but it beat suffocating.

Stars filled the screen now. They were completely out of the Pitch.

Kelis hissed a curse. "At least one shuttle remains in range."

"Where? I'm not reading it on our sensors." Tension filled Stag's voice.

"I can only see it because one of the trackers attached. It's almost out of this system, but it's there. Nothing on the second shuttle."

"We tagged one of them." Hellion suddenly lifted his hand and made a fist. "Yes!"

Nala opened her mouth but then closed it. *What tracker?*

"They must not have detected it. Good. Show it on the main." Stag leaned forward a little in his chair. "They're probably traveling together."

A blip flashed to the far right of the screen.

"We hope," Hellion muttered.

"Silence," Stag demanded. "We'll keep this speed until they are out of range, then get out of here."

"Home," Kelis muttered. "I'll be happy to see it."

Nala saw some of the cyborgs smile. They might be thrilled to be returning to wherever they lived, but she wasn't. At least on this ship, she knew she'd be with Stag. Once they docked with their station or landed on a planet, she had no idea what would happen to her.

She closed her eyes and took a deep breath, blowing it. Life had taught her to tackle one problem at a time. She was strong. Whatever awaited her, she'd deal with it. She was a survivor.

Chapter Ten

Stag watched Nala take a seat on the bed they shared. The past few hours had been tense. The Markus Model shuttle they were able to track had gone out of sensor range and now the *Varnish* traveled toward Garden. Veller would wake him if anything happened. The male was an accomplished replacement to take the helm. He had faith in his abilities.

"You spoke."

She arched her eyebrows. "Sorry."

"You promised you wouldn't."

"I'm human. Sue me. I was dying of curiosity. Why the full burns and drastic stops?"

"I had my reasons."

"Mind sharing them? Please? I remember you like that word..."

He bent, tugging off his boots. "The Markus Models dispensed bombs inside the dead zone."

Shock flashed across her features. "They mined the Pitch? Shit!"

"The types they used are drawn to vessel hulls. I didn't want them attaching to us."

"You wanted to outrun them so they'd have a harder time of locking on." She removed the socks she kept taking from his drawer, baring her feet. "Damn, you're smart."

"I'm a cyborg."

"I thought you were crazy. I would have blown up part of my ship if I'd pulled a stunt like that with the *Pride*. She was old though. She rattled and almost shook apart the last time I had to race her. I'd never have dared to full blast from a dead takeoff. I had to slowly increase speeds to keep her in one piece."

"Why did you go to that speed if it wasn't something your freighter could handle?"

"Pirates. They were the bane of my existence. We could always outrun them but I swear they've gotten smarter in the last year. It used to be that we'd run across a single ship and it put off enough radiation that our sensors detected them long-range. We'd adjust course and increase speed a bit so they didn't stand a chance of catching us. Four months ago, six of their ships were working together, or they were just closely spaced apart. It kind of caused a net effect. We had to push the *Pride* harder than I'd ever done before. They got close enough to fire on us that time. They missed, but it got hairy."

He put his boots away in the drawer and turned. "Hairy?"

"Scary. Close call." She shrugged. "Never heard that term before, huh? They almost got us. I was actually worried that time."

"They wanted the sex bots you were transporting?"

"There's no way they knew. It was a secret. I didn't want a target on my back. Lots of thieves would have searched for us if they knew what we were carrying. Those bots are worth big credits on the black market. Pirates target anything large enough to carry food supplies, and the *Pride* probably looked like they'd hit the jackpot. Imagine their surprise if they'd actually boarded us to steal food." She smirked.

"Your job was dangerous."

"What job isn't these days when you work in space?"

He couldn't deny the truth in her words. "Most women don't venture this far out. It's considered lawless. Earth Government rarely sends battle cruisers beyond the Baylor System."

"It's too costly to resupply them beyond that point. I know. It would have taken my freighter three trips to Earth and back just for the food staples they use up with a crew that size. Think of the time involved. They would need a fleet of transports hauling water, food, spare parts, and other essentials to them every few months to keep a battle cruiser stocked if they regularly patrolled this far out. Imagine the fuel they'd need, too. Some of those vessels carry five to eight hundred crew members."

He crossed the room and took a seat next to her. "I never thought of that."

"It's my job to know about supplies and shipping them." She smiled. "The battle cruisers that do venture this far out are here to blow something up, then return back to Earth. They're already stocked enough to last that length of trip without needing to be resupplied."

"Blow something up?"

"Like the Chandler Station."

He hadn't heard of it. His expression must have shown that.

"It was only open for four weeks. It was this station that flew to the Spacian sector. Some hotshot funded it, thinking he could make a fortune off pirates. That was the word going around, anyway. Full facility, for black-market trading and doing ship repairs. *Any* ship repairs. Anyone who could pay the credits, and they didn't care if the ship was sanctioned or not. Some of us captains were excited because the closest station with repair bays is on the Arris." She shuddered. "Let's say we avoided that one. It's got a bad reputation for violence. They might allow pirates to dock, but no repairs are offered to them, so EG left them alone. The Chandler Station, on the other hand, said fuck you to EG from the get-go. They were advertising before they even set up in the sector."

"So the Earth Government...?"

She nodded. "They sent out a battle cruiser and blew it to hell. No more Chandler Station. I heard they put up a fight, even got some pirate ships to defend them, but they didn't stand a chance. Only a few ships got out of there intact. My dad talked to one of the captains, another hauler, and he swore they had him dead to rights but let him go. He's registered, so he guessed that's why he survived. Dad thought it was more a case of EG wanting word to spread that they don't take that kind of shit, and not to mess with them."

"What does being registered matter?"

"We have to pay a percentage of all our profits to EG. I was registered with them. They took twenty percent from me. The stations pay thirty percent or higher, depending on their size and income. It's the difference between being a sanctioned business and being seen as a criminal breaking the law. Get it?"

"I do." He intensely disliked Earth Government.

"They screw you either way, but at least paying them keeps us from being fired on or imprisoned. On Earth, they take far more from businesses. My grandfather got screwed out of half his profits."

"What did he do?"

"Import business. He dealt in selling furnishings for those luxury liners. EG stole his business from me two days after he died." Her voice reflected her anger. "They took over the contracts, stationed guards around the warehouses where we stored our merchandise, and told all our employees to leave or they'd be shot."

"They could do that?"

"EG never asks. Comply or die. It's how it is. I got the hell out of there before they decided to empty his credit accounts and seize his house, too. I sold it, drained the accounts, and bought the *Pride*."

"Do you miss Earth?"

She seemed to consider it. "Living on a planet and breathing fresh air? Sure. But that's not worth living with Earth Government. I've done some supply drops to a few colony planets, just three, but they weren't ideal either. You know?"

"I don't. Explain."

"Bram is so hot. The city is mostly underground. You can go up at night when the sun isn't baking the surface but it's really barren. The air felt weird too, very dry and heavy. It's the same with Scorch. They named that one appropriately. It's a hundred and fifty degrees in the shade when the surface is exposed to their sun, but there's a lot of water underground. Tons of cavern systems. It's pretty but who wants to live in...well, water caves? Ever been?"

"No."

"They built on the water because while the surface is dry, it's too hot. And rivers are veined everywhere under the ground. There are very few accessible underground surfaces not covered in water. They build everything boat style."

"It sounds fascinating."

"It was great to visit but I wouldn't want to live there."

"And the third?" He was curious, enjoyed watching her facial expressions as she talked. She didn't attempt to hide her emotions.

"Klaus is too cold." She hugged her arms, as if the memory made her chilled. "It snows year round. They joked it was named after Santa Claus, just using a K instead because of the trees. They lost about fifty people when they first settled there, before they figured it out. Killer trees. No thanks."

That surprised him. "How did colonists die because of the trees? Were they poisonous?"

"The trees are alive. They eat anything they can grab. People included. I thought they were joking, you know, messing with the tourists, but the guy I delivered supplies to showed me a vid of one of the trees snatching up some of the local wildlife. The damn thing threw out a branch, grabbed up one of the hundred-pound sheep-looking beast that roams the surface, and the trunk opened. It shoved the poor thing inside it. Dinner was served. They're rooted to the ground but the limbs can move and the trunks bend. He told me to stay at least three hundred yards away from them to be safe."

"Are they sentient?"

"Who cares? Did you miss the part where they eat people?"

"I was wondering if they could communicate. They might see the colonists as invaders to their planet. The trees might act in self-defense, rather than viewing it as murder."

She grinned. "You're so cute. Look at you thinking of the poor trees."

"It's a valid point."

"It is." Her smile remained. "What if they *are* sentient? Would you go hug a tree and make friends?"

He narrowed his eyes, studying her. "Are you mocking me?"

"No, but I *am* amused. You hear about killer trees and you're thinking about their motives. I didn't care why they ate people. It just freaked me out, and I couldn't fly out of there fast enough. What a horrible way to go. No thanks."

"We have life forms on the planet we settled on, and we live in peace with them."

"Are they killer trees?" She sobered, fear showing in her eyes.

"No. They are amphibian-humanoid life forms with intelligence. We built our city away from their ocean, on land, where they don't seem to venture much. It was paramount to us not to make them feel threatened or invaded by our presence."

Nala liked the way Stag spoke about the aliens. "You care about them."

"Of course. I'm certain they were afraid when we first landed on the surface and they became aware of us. We went out of our way to show no aggression and establish communications, but they ran from us. We set up a camp near the beach, allowed them to watch and learn about us, hoping they'd finally approach. They didn't as the weeks passed. We used the time to learn where they avoided travel, did terrestrial scans to make certain nothing under the ground was a danger, and chose that location to settle our city."

"Nice." It really was. "How are they situated technology wise?"

He shook his head. "They don't seem to have any."

That stunned her. "None?"

"We've done some scans with fly drones at a distance but didn't want to be too invasive, to avoid frightening them. They have built small cities under water and in caves near the beaches. They are impressive designs, but we've never picked up any indication that they are far advanced. They have lighting though. It could be from a natural source. We detected some lava tubes under the ocean floor in the shallow parts where they habitat."

"So you just let them be?"

"You sound surprised." His tone took on a sharp edge.

She fought the urge to touch him but didn't dare. "Don't pick a fight with me. You tend to do that. It's just that most people who settle on planets aren't so courteous of the local inhabitants."

"You mean *Earthers* do that."

He spat that title, making it clear it was an insult. She decided to tackle the issue head-on. "Enough. I'm not your enemy, Stag. EG screwed me over too. No, I wasn't enslaved or created by them. Did you hear me when I said they stole my grandfather's company? Running it was supposed to be my future. They took that away. I could be bitter and angry, but I chose to seek an adventure instead. I bought a freighter and flew into space."

He just watched her. She hated noticing how his long and dark eyelashes really made the blue of his eyes appear breathtaking. She liked him a little too much, and actually found his prickly personality a bit appealing. She always knew where she stood with Stag.

The evening before flashed, and so did the earlier conversation they'd had before leaving his quarters.

Stag broke the silence. "You *should* hate Earth Government. They are responsible for you leaving your home planet, and they created the Markus Models that attacked your ship."

"Wow. Ever heard of looking for a bright side? I got to spend just over six years with my dad. I wouldn't trade that time for anything. He never would have retired or left the military if I'd stayed on Earth. He hated even visiting there."

"Now he's dead, and you're left with nothing."

That hurt. She turned her head away, staring at her lap. "Thanks for pointing that out."

"Nala," he rasped. "I apologize." He reached over and rested his hand on the small of her back. "You will be treated well by our council. They are nothing similar to your government."

She lowered her head. "Yeah. Sure. If being forced into sexual slavery and given to some guy translates into being 'treated well'. Sounds fun. That's sarcasm, by the way. And at least now I know it's a planet. I wasn't sure where you were taking me."

"Garden is beautiful, and the weather is favorable year round. The trees won't attack you. The name we gave it is an accurate description."

She looked at him. "Will I ever see you again once you dump me there?"

"The city isn't that large. I'm certain we'll meet again when I'm on the planet's surface."

"You spend most of your time in space?"

"Yes. This shuttle is mine. I volunteer for all the dangerous missions."

"Adrenaline junkie?"

"No. I don't seek excitement and danger to enhance my life experiences."

"Then why do you do it?"

"Someone has to."

"You have a hero complex, don't you?"

"No."

"A death wish?"

He hesitated a little before answering. "I'm not in a family unit, nor do I have many close associations to other cyborgs. I'm expendable."

It caused her chest to ache. He really believed that. She could see the sincerity in his eyes. Had anyone ever loved Stag? She doubted it.

"I'd grieve you, so don't get yourself killed."

He pulled his hand away. "Those are polite words but spare them for someone else."

"Now you're breaking my heart." She turned on the bed, inching closer to him. "We've been intimate. I don't hate you, Stag. Sure, sometimes I'd like to strangle you. You're tough to get close to but you're a good man. I wouldn't kill you." She grinned. "Just a little choking would be involved if you really pissed me off, but I'd stop before I really hurt you."

"Sexual intimacy means nothing."

Again, his words stung. "Ouch. Well, I'm not you. It meant something to *me*. I can't compartmentalize my body from my feelings. Sorry. You die, I'm going to cry. Deal with that."

That seemed to either irritate him or make him uncomfortable. "Go to sleep."

She frowned. "I thought you wanted me to—"

"No," he cut her off. "This ends now."

She studied his handsome face and the way he looked at her. "You're starting to feel things for me, aren't you? Afraid?"

150

He glared.

"I'll take that for a yes."

"You don't frighten me, Earther."

"Right. And stop calling me that. I think you've spent a lifetime, however long that is, keeping everyone distanced. You admitted you don't have many friends and spend all your time on this ship. You don't want anyone to care too much about you because then you might feel something back. You make me sad, Stag."

"Go to sleep."

"Do you plan to tie me up again?"

"You're no threat. Just stay near the wall and don't touch me."

The rejection hurt. So did the fact that he wasn't ever going to let her get close to him again, emotionally or physically. Part of her wished she could hate him, but she wouldn't have that ache in her chest if that were possible. Stag might be prickly and remote, but she'd seen traits in him that had softened her heart toward him.

"Fine."

"I no longer wish to talk to you." He stood. "I need to check on something."

She watched him leave. It was more like fleeing.

She cursed, lay down, and scooted all the way over against the wall. Tears filled her eyes and she let them flow.

Maybe she'd allowed herself to feel for him only because she'd lost everything else in her life.

Chapter Eleven

Stag wiped sealing gel off his hands, staring at Kelis. "Well?"

The cyborg checked the sensors and nodded. "Pressure seems to be holding. We'll know for certain after the engines start."

"I wonder what else can go wrong?" Hellion closed one of the electronic ports and sighed. "This has to be the worst mission we've been on."

"I wouldn't go that far." Kelis kept his focus on the pad he held. "Remember that colony ship we found adrift? I still have nightmares about that."

Stag grimaced. "I try to forget."

"What are we talking about?" Maze entered the engine room.

"The ship where the colonists went nuts and slaughtered each other," Hellion answered. "We had to clean up bodies for days so we could haul it back to Garden for them to salvage."

"I thought we decided to never bring that up again." Maze handed out water and a power bar to each man. "Drink and eat. You've been down here for six hours without taking a break. What reminded you of that ship?"

"Hellion believes this has to be our worst mission." Kelis put away the pad and opened the energy bar, taking a bite. "I disagree. We were able to blow up the *Pride*, didn't have to scrape up decaying bodies, or haul that thing back to Garden. We did escape the dead zone. This

152

flooding mess wasn't as bad as body removal and it didn't involve wearing suits to avoid a putrid smell."

Stag thought of Nala as he ate the bar and drank his water. She'd loved the *Pride*. He wondered what she'd have thought of having her freighter salvaged for building supplies on Garden, rather than being blown up. He was glad he never had to find out. Her crew and father had died aboard. It was probably best that she never had any kind of reminder of that once she reached the planet.

"Let's hope nothing else goes wrong." Hellion took a seat on the case containing all the damaged wiring he'd had to replace.

"Did you feed our guest?" Stag addressed Maze.

"Of course. She claimed you've been avoiding her."

"I've spent most of my time down here sorting this mess." He hated the way he felt he needed to defend his actions as the males all gave him questioning looks. "The line ruptured and flooded out this section. I wanted to personally be on hand for all the repairs."

"Every wire, circuit, and filter had to be switched out for new ones," Hellion grumbled. "I found damage in all the panels. I also replaced the seals so they won't leak if this ever happens again. Stag and I have practically had to live here."

"Exactly," Stag said, feeling grateful the male took his side. "The engine fluid caused erosion, since the pumps were slow to drain out the section. I fixed those too."

"I told you I could help out more."

Stag hid his irritation with Kelis. "Your skills were better used in Control monitoring for any signs of the Markus Models searching for us."

"Maze could have monitored the sensors since shuttle repair isn't his forte. We're moving slow enough for their sensors to misread us."

"Perhaps they adjusted their sensors. We can't take that chance. It's logical for them to assume we suffered severe damage at a minimum if we escaped dead space after they set those bombs. We'd be slow moving or have to find a place to hole up to do repairs. I want someone in charge of Control who is skilled with battle tactics if needed." Stag glanced at the medic. "We're also in pirate territory. You might hesitate to fire on them, since they're known to take female captives. You'd feel sorry for any innocents aboard their ships. No offense, but I wouldn't put you in that position."

"None taken." Maze smiled. "I never want to take your seat, Stag. I don't want to make those difficult decisions."

A beep sounded and Stag turned on coms. "Status?"

"Nothing to report but you wanted an update every two hours," Veller stated. "We aren't picking up any traffic in this system."

"You have excellent timing. Repairs are finished. Start engine two, but baby it. Compensate for the difference with thrusters." Stag motioned the men in the room to move toward the door to a safe spot in case any of the seals blew. "We may as well test them now while we're in communication."

A loud hum began and Stag relaxed within minutes when nothing went wrong. He smiled. "Let's go home, Veller. I'm on my way to you."

154

He nodded at his men and left fast, done with the conversation. He knew he'd avoided Nala and didn't need his crew giving him any crap about it. They wouldn't understand how unsettling his last conversation with her had been.

He stopped in one of the crew quarters quickly and used the cleansing unit, then borrowed an outfit from Hellion's storage.

He reached Control five minutes later. Veller stood and moved out of his seat. Stag dropped into his chair, placing his palm over the pad. The screen in front of him showed open space.

Then the sensors almost instantly detected six ships.

Stag wanted to punch something. "Where the hell did all of them come from?"

"Shit!" Veller moved fast, taking the weapons station. "Pirates."

"I'm reading the radiation signatures too." Stag opened coms ship-wide to his crew. "Get to Control *now*."

"There shouldn't be so many." Veller sounded stunned. "Where did they come from so fast? Were they hiding behind the dead planets?"

"It appears so." Stag evaluated the other ships, their placement, and put the *Varnish* on high alert when the other ships began to head in their direction. Red lights flashed at the back of the room. "They laid in wait for a ship to come and now are engaging. It seems we're in for a fight."

"We're under orders to avoid conflict if possible," Veller reminded him. "We should attempt to outrun them."

"The seals are still hardening. We could lose engine two if we put that much pressure on that new fluid line. We can't risk it going down and losing power to a main thruster." Stag changed course. "There are only two ships in this direction. Target them as soon as we're in range. We just need to stay ahead of the group until it's safe to full burn." He mentally calculated how much time it would take. "We have to keep out of their weapon range for five hours."

Veller grumbled something but it wasn't loud enough to hear.

"What was that?"

Veller twisted to face him. "We could still outrun them if engine two goes down."

"We could," Stag agreed. "But if we lose engine one, we'd come to a full stop and lose all power, including two weapons. I'm not willing to take that risk."

"I don't foresee that happening."

"Did you foresee engine two going down five days ago? I'm certain the stress fractures were caused by our maneuvers out of the dead zone. We scanned but they didn't show until the leaks happened. The same could happen with engine one."

Veller's mouth compressed into a tight line and he faced his station. "Understood."

Stag regretted snapping at him. They were all under stress, wanted to return to Garden, and being slowed down by repairs always frustrated his crew. He adjusted his tone to a calmer, more neutral one.

"Part of my duty is to take everything into account. We're heavily outnumbered and now is not the time to take any unnecessary risks. It's best to be cautious. We'll damage the two ships, keep ahead of the four trailing us, and outrun them when we're certain the fixed fluid line can hold the pressure going through it."

Veller glanced at him and nodded. "You're right."

The doors to Control opened and Hellion, Kelis, and Maze entered. Maze spoke first. "Parqel and Yammer are sleeping. Should I wake them?"

"No." Stag changed course again. "Take stations. Maze, you're not needed here. I want you back in the engine room watching those new seals. Alert us if they begin to leak."

"Understood." Maze spun around and left.

Kelis grunted. "The pirates seem organized."

"They do," Hellion agreed. "It's like they're communicating with each other and working as a team."

Another blip showed on sensors. Stag fisted his hand. "There are seven of them now. They are attempting to surround us."

"We should inform the *Star*." Veller glanced at him. "It could be a decoy to lead them from us. Pirates would love to engage a vessel that large."

"I spoke to Flint four days ago. One of our warning sensors went off in the Ovis System. They went to check out what is there."

"That puts them too far from us."

"Thank you for pointing out the obvious, Hellion." Stag scowled. "We'll still take out the two ships ahead of us and clear a path. They can trail us. We're fast enough to stay ahead of them. Otherwise, we'll turn and take them out one by one. We are better at targeting."

"We have important cargo onboard and have suffered some damage. A battle isn't in our best interest."

Stag glared at Veller, getting irritated with his constant opinions. "I'm in charge. Shut up or leave Control. I refuse to argue with you."

Veller appeared stunned.

Stag hated being questioned as captain but it was no excuse for snapping at his crew. He cleared his throat. "We'll target the ones in front of us and leave a wide spread debris field in our wake. It will slow the other pirates while we increase speed, get out of sensor range, and change course." He dropped his gaze to his pad. "Then we'll head home. They'll lose us and won't be able to communicate our location to others." It would mean he had a few more days before he could hand Nala over to the council on Garden.

"Agreed but I think we should attempt to speed past them without firing. They are slower than we are." Veller faced forward. "They're usually bad at targeting us."

"I'm not willing to chance it in case they get lucky. We target the two ships coming at us before they get too close to fire upon us. Stow your suggestions, Veller. Enough."

Stag fumed. He understood Veller believed it was his duty to point out other solutions to any problems they faced, but he currently wasn't in

158

the mood for it. He hadn't slept much in the past five days, his mind on Nala far too often.

* * * * *

Nala sat up on the bed when she heard a slight rumble. A few seconds later, another one followed. She climbed out of bed, walked to the panel next to the door, and pressed her hand on it. "Maze? Is this connection still active?"

Seconds passed before the medic answered. "I never revoked it. Is something wrong, Nala?"

"What's that sound I just heard?"

"Weapons fire."

"We're being attacked?" Dread hit fast and hard. "The skin droids?"

"Pirates."

She flinched. "Shit."

"Do not worry." His voice sounded calm enough. "We've had to deal with plenty of pirates over the years. We've never suffered any losses."

"Why not just outrun them? That's what we always did on the *Pride*."

"We completed engine two repairs but the seals are new."

She understood what that meant. "We can't full burn. The pressure might blow them out until they have time to fully set."

"Yes. I'm in engine room two at this moment watching them."

"Any leaks?"

"None yet."

159

"Where is Stag? At the helm?"

"Of course."

She hung her head, knowing that had been a stupid question, but she hadn't seen him for more than a few minutes in quite a while. He would come in to get a fresh uniform, then leave. She'd lost track of the days. "Are we going to be okay? I mean, are we in danger?"

"From pirates? No. It's more of an annoyance."

A rumble sounded and she lifted her head, staring around the small quarters. "Did we just fire again?"

"Yes. I'm monitoring Control. One pirate ship has been completely disabled and another damaged. We will fire on it again as we pass."

"Pass?"

"Stag's plan is to fire upon the two in our path and allow the rest to trail us until we can full burn safely. That should be in about five hours. Relax, Nala. Stress is bad for you and we have this situation in hand."

Another rumble sounded. "How many more ships are out there?"

He paused. "Six now, minus the two we've disabled."

Eight pirate ships? She felt fear, despite what Maze told her. "They're attempting to swarm us?"

"I'm not familiar with that term."

"Can you connect me to Stag? I need to talk to him."

He hesitated.

"Damn it, Maze!" Her temper flared. "I get reports regularly from other ships that are attacked by pirates. Mass attacks are something

160

they've been doing lately. Chances are, that's what's about to happen. If that's the case, a hell of a lot more of them are going to show up. They even connect their ships together so on sensors it reads as one large ship, then they undock and spread apart. They'll attempt to net us in and then open fire once we're surrounded. Get it? Connect me with Stag."

"We had a ship witness that behavior once. Pirates attacked a carrier. It was thought to be a singular occurrence."

"It used to be, but not anymore. Connect me to Stag."

"I'll give him the information you've shared."

"I want to talk to him. I know what to do."

"He will contact you if he wants your input. Maze out."

"Don't disconnect!" she demanded. Seconds ticked by. "Maze?"

She cursed, jerking her hand off the panel. He'd cut her off. "Goddamn cyborgs! They think they're so smart." She paced the floor, hoping Stag would com her. Minutes passed by and she realized he wouldn't. She stepped over to the door and placed her palm on the panel. "Maze? Answer."

"I'm busy, Nala."

She felt relief that he didn't block her. "Listen to me. Tell Stag he *has* to risk blowing the new seals. There've been at least ten freighters who have been attacked in a swarm pattern over the past few months. We're talking twenty-plus pirate ships that show up. Do you hear me? They're transmitting our location to all the pirates in surrounding areas and they will come at us from all sides if they're able to! We *have* to get off their sensors and change course as fast as possible. Those bastards are working together now."

"I'll relay the message. Maze out."

She fumed when he cut her off again.

Nala continued to pace, hoping Stag would take her advice. Otherwise, they might be in a world of shit.

Stag ended his conversation with Maze and grimly read the sensors. Two more blips showed up on long-range. Seconds later, another ship registered. It seemed Nala knew what she was talking about. He leaned back in his chair. "Prepare to full burn."

Veller turned in his seat, his mouth opening.

"Don't say a word. New information has come to light. We need to get out of this sector now. We're being boxed in and more pirates are on their way to us. They plan a full-scale attack." He opened up the charts of the sectors around them, scanning for a place to disappear. A belt of asteroids caught his attention. He adjusted course to the sector next it and opened coms to Maze. "Watch those seals closely." He cut coms and did an override to Yammer's quarters, ordering the male to get out of bed and rush to engine one to watch for any problems.

He waited until they passed the damaged pirate ships they'd targeted and then took over the helm, controlling their speed himself. He'd had it with Veller, and didn't want his authority questioned again.

162

"Mark on zero," he announced. "Three, two, one." He didn't go to full burn at first, but instead increased power to the thrusters steadily, until they were at maximum capacity.

Yammer reported reaching the engine room and wasn't seeing any signs of pressure leaks. Stag hoped that news remained the same. Minutes later, Maze contacted him.

"We have one minor leak. I'm attempting to seal it."

"I'm sending Parqel to assist you."

He woke the other crew member and studied the long-range sensors. They were leaving the pirate ships behind, and only a few new ships tried to intercept them. He changed course when the screen cleared and headed toward the asteroid belt.

Hellion cleared his throat. "The abandoned mining core sample?"

His crew knew him well. "Yes."

"The heavy metals inside the largest rock will mess with our sensors but it will hide us from theirs too." A wide smile spread across Hellion's face. "They won't look there. It's a bitch to maneuver that far into the belt without being smashed apart by the smaller chunks. We can easily do it, but they can't."

He nodded. "I doubt they are aware that Earth Government took core samples twenty years ago. That sector was too monitored at the time by patrol ships."

"I disagree," Veller stated. "Earth stopped having that sector patrolled as soon as they decided there wasn't anything they wanted there any longer. The pirates have had at least a decade to get to know that belt. We should keep at this speed and return home, not find a hole to hide in."

The cyborg got on Stag's last nerve. "We also have a leak in engine two, which could take that engine down if more open up. I'm not willing to risk it. We going to find a safe spot and do patches. What is your problem? You're pissing me off!"

"You're not the only one feeling anger. I'm excellent at repairs, yet you made me sit for five shifts in a row watching readings. What have I done to raise your contempt or make you believe I'm incompetent?"

Stag tried to hide his surprise.

"You've always allowed me to head repairs. I must have done something to lose your trust. I know you appreciate strong males who have excellent leadership skills. Perhaps I've grown lax in my duty. I'm attempting to show you that's not so."

Stag held his gaze. He hadn't meant for Veller to take it that way. He glanced at his crew in Control. All of them were watching him. They'd spent years together, were a tight group, and he had to admit his recent behavior might have been taken wrong.

"I needed the distraction. It had nothing to do with you, Veller. I have been avoiding spending much time in my quarters," he admitted. "I left you in charge of Control because I trust you that much."

Veller's tense expression cleared. "The Earther."

"Yes. I apologize. I should have stated that right off."

"Only you wouldn't." Hellion had the nerve to chuckle. "You don't like to share your feelings. Nala is getting to you, isn't she?"

"I refuse to discuss this. We're on alert right now. Focus on the problems at hand." Stag lowered his gaze to the screen. "We're clear of pirates." He adjusted course again. "Let's get lost while we're out of sight of them."

"She is *hot*. I would let her pretend I was a sex bot and take any orders she gave if it meant getting her naked in my bed." Hellion made a low growling sound. "I don't blame you for finally realizing she's appealing and distancing yourself. I'd be all over her in your place."

Kelis snorted. "Yes, you would, but the rest of us have more control over our body functions."

Stag refused to look away from his pad, memories of Nala naked in his bed filling his thoughts. Most of his crew would be disappointed if they ever learned he'd been unable to resist the Earther's sex appeal. He was supposed to set an example for them, and he'd failed.

He really needed to reach Garden so he could hand her over to the council.

Chapter Twelve

Stag targeted a chunk of rock, tethering the last cable to the side wall of the inner core of the massive asteroid. There was slight gravity inside but not enough for the shuttle to remain in one place without the lines. They'd made it inside without any exterior damage. It had been a tight fit to back into the huge circular hole some mining operation had blasted tens of thousands of feet deep into the slow-spinning mountain of rock.

"I've got weapons targeted and ready to fire if anything shows up at the opening," Kelis stated.

"Just make certain you fire at them *before* they enter." Hellion shuddered. "I don't want to be buried if the walls collapse. There's no exit. That's the only way in or out of this cavern."

"Stow your emotions," Stag ordered.

Hellion turned in his seat. "Am I the only one who hates being in a big dark hole? We could block the opening by accident if another vessel slams into it, and become trapped. The heavy metals not only block sensors but we'd be unable to call for help. Coms don't work in here except ship-wide."

A headache began to form. Stag reached up and rubbed his temple. He used his other hand to form a link with both engine rooms. "Parqel? Status."

"We only suffered the one leak and it was minor. We've resealed it and it's holding now that the engines are powered down."

"I've already cleaned up the slight spillage," Maze added.

"Good." Stag sighed. "Yammer? Report."

"All readings are fine. I've visually inspected everything. No leaks. The pressure reads a little high on one line but it held."

"Will it last until we reach Garden? Best assessment."

"I believe so. We'll just have to watch it closely."

"Thank you, Yammer. All of you may return to quarters until your shifts start." He closed coms and stood, stretching after being in his seat for too long. "Now we wait it out to make certain the pirates haven't managed to track us."

"What if they did?" Hellion scowled at him.

"They have to come at us head-on, one at a time. That opening isn't large enough to fit two vessels." Stag shrugged. "It makes them easier to kill. Besides, a lot of them would be taken out in the asteroid belt just to get this deep. They don't have the hull shielding we do and some of those small fragments hit us. We didn't suffer damage but they won't be able to claim the same."

"It was a logical choice," Veller stated.

Stag flashed him a look but said nothing. At least the male wasn't questioning his every move now. That made things a bit easier and less infuriating.

"You appear tired. Do you want me to take your chair while you get some rest? Nothing is going to happen over the next few hours. It would take that long for the pirates to catch up, if they were able to track us."

Stag appreciated the concern Veller showed now that they'd resolved their issue, but he shook his head. Resting would mean returning to his quarters—and Nala. Or worse, borrowing a bunk from one of the men in Control while they were on shift. He hoped Hellion hadn't noticed he'd taken one of his uniforms. The male didn't call him on if he had.

"I'm good."

"The chances of the pirates finding us are—"

Stag wanted to punch him. "Stow it, Hellion! Slim to none. Let's leave it at that. They may do a search pattern and will give up within two days. We'll stay here, then venture out a bit to read sensors once we're clear of the belt."

"I'll be glad when this mission is over. I still believe this is the worst one yet. Now we've had to run from pirates. I'll take dead body cleanup any day over feeling as if I'm a coward."

Stag clenched his teeth. "Hellion…"

"I know. Stow it and stop being emotional." Hellion sighed, facing forward. "This is going to be boring. I almost wish I were still doing repairs. At least the time flew by."

Stag's headache grew worse. It was a combination of lack of sleep, stress, physical exhaustion, and he hadn't eaten a full meal in days. He retook his seat, staring at the screen. They were in a dark mass with the opening ahead. Large chunks of rocks floated by, the belt always moving them in rotation. It encircled an inhabitable planet.

His thoughts returned to Nala. She always lingered in the back of his mind, and it annoyed him. Part of him wanted nothing more than to go spend time with her. His dick responded by getting semi erect.

He closed his eyes, rubbed his temple again, and tried to forget what it felt like to be inside her.

He'd had sex with females plenty of times when he'd been auditioning to join a family unit. It had been right after they'd reached Garden and begun to build the city. None of those women had responded to him the way the Earther did. Cyborgs could be cold, remote, and they easily masked their emotions. They didn't moan and thrash under him, nor dig their fingernails into his skin. He had to admit, it made sex more intense and pleasurable.

"Odd."

Kelis's soft murmur drew him from his thoughts. Stag opened his eyes and placed his hand on the pad, trying to figure out what was wrong. He detected an alarm going off on one of the docking doors located in cargo hold two. The other sensors didn't detect another ship, which mean the seal might be compromised.

"A malfunction? Perhaps one of the debris hits we took did damage after all." Veller stood. "I'll go check it out."

"Put on a suit before entering the cargo hold," Stag ordered. "In case of a rupture. Do an exterior examination. The crates we took onboard have been stowed. They won't float if you exit that hatch."

"Are you reading this?" Hellion's voice deepened with stress. "The oxygen levels in cargo two have increased."

Stag did, almost coming out of his chair. The oxygen levels were higher than normal. He instantly turned on the warning system to go ship-wide and opened all coms. "We're being breached. Red alert! Arm yourselves."

"It has to be a sensor error." Veller rushed to the weapons panel though, collecting laser pistols, stunners, and the high-voltage weapons for each crew member. He passed them out with haste.

"Increased oxygen levels mean the motion sensors were triggered. We purposely shut down those areas if nothing alive is inside. Those sensors are reading bodies—moving ones." Stag stood, holstering the weapons to his uniform belt. "Where the hell did they come from?"

"They had to already be inside the crater and we weren't aware of the other ship. Our sensors are blind but they must have seen us." Kelis paused by the door. "Life signs onboard?"

"Fifteen," Hellion rasped. "That's seven more than there should be. We have been boarded."

Stag contacted Maze. "Get to my quarters. Protect Nala. We have seven intruders. Origins unknown."

"I'm on my way."

"Don't hesitate to fire on them," Stag snarled. "Do you hear me? They are hostile, or they wouldn't have boarded us without permission."

The medic took a second too long to answer. "Understood."

"Yammer? Parqel? Report. Did you hear the alarm?"

"Yes," both of them replied. Then Yammer continued, "We're armed. Orders?"

"Seven hostiles. They entered by cargo two. Locate and take them out. We're on our way."

Stag pointed to Kelis. "You have Control. Watch the entrance so we don't have more company. Fire if you see any ships. Hellion, guard the door. Seal it once we're out." He spun, storming to the exit. "You're with me, Veller."

"This *is* the worst mission," Hellion called out.

* * * * *

Nala lay on the bed facing the wall when the doors slid open. "It's about time!" She rolled, expecting to give Stag a piece of her mind.

Maze entered her room and the doors sealed behind him. He slapped his palm on the pad next to it. She took note of the weapon in his hand. That was a first. He usually only carried a tray of food or his medical kit.

She sat up and scooted to the edge of the bed, swinging her legs off. "What's wrong?"

"We've been boarded."

That shocked her into silence.

"Seven new life signs are aboard the *Varnish*. We're not certain if they are human, pirates, or Markus Models."

Her surprise turned to terror and she got to her feet. "Skin droids? Do you have a spare weapon?"

He turned his head, peering at her. "I only have the one, and it wouldn't do much good even if we fired upon them. They are difficult to damage. I don't have the right kind of weapon."

"What does that mean?"

"They can only be killed by high voltages of electricity. I don't exactly keep that kind of weapon inside my quarters. Control has them though. I just have my laser."

That didn't sound good at all. "Can you track the signals? Do you have monitoring equipment?"

"No vid monitoring. We can track life signs. They have passed through cargo hold two and have entered the shuttle. They have broken into two teams of two, and one of three." He paused. "They are splitting up, two going to engine room one, the three-man team is accessing the lift to reach Control..." His eyes widened. "Two life signs are heading this way, toward crew quarters."

Nala tried not to panic. "Life signs. That means they aren't skin droids. I mean, we didn't pick up any extras on our ship when they attacked us." She tensed, lifting one arm and holding out her hand. "We can handle pirates. Give me the weapon."

He shook his head.

"Come on! You're big and strong. You can totally kick pirate ass. You deck one, I'll shoot the other. That's a good plan."

He released the panel and backed away from the door. "Find cover."

She glanced around the small area. "There *is* none." Her attention focused on the cleansing unit.

172

Maze followed her gaze. "I don't want you to be where I am. They won't fire on you if they are pirates. They'll want to keep you alive. But they may accidently hit you in battle if you're too close to me. Get on the other side of the bed and crouch down."

"It's a bunk. They are totally going to see me."

He accessed the cleansing unit, stepped inside, and kept the door open. Part of the wall shielded his body. "I'm aware. You will distract them."

"Great." She did as she was told, going to the far side of the bunk and crouching. She could see over the top and kept her eyes trained on the door.

"Stag and the crew are on their way. We just need to hold on long enough for them to eliminate the threat."

"The bad guys may not be able to breach that door."

Maze dashed her hopes. "They've already breached two crew quarters."

"How do you know?"

"I kept my link with the computer." He suddenly gasped and the lights in the room went out.

"What was that?" She couldn't see a thing.

"I believe they just sabotaged something in engine room one and knocked out power. My link is broken."

Emergency lighting came on but it was faint and gave a weird, eerie red tinge to the room. A popping noise sounded by the door, and Nala gripped the edge of the bunk as metal groaned and the doors began to open. Whoever was out there had some kind of tool that slowly pried them open. She could see well enough to make out the weapon, gloved hand, and uniform of the person who attempted to enter the room.

The uniform colors were instantly identifiable.

Maze fired his weapon and hit his target. The soldier's body flew backward, out of sight into the hallway with a loud thud.

A piercing whine sounded and Nala threw her hands over her ears, shoved her chin down against her chest, and closed her eyes.

The huge boom and bright flash that came a second later threw her painfully against the wall, knocking the air from her lungs on impact. Her bent legs gave out under her and she landed on her butt.

It took her precious seconds to remember how to breathe before she opened her eyes, lifted her head, and released her ears. The second soldier had entered the room and had his weapon shifting from her to the damaged cleansing unit.

"Don't shoot!" She raised her hands, palms showing, and spread her fingers apart. "I'm unarmed."

The soldier held her gaze and then stepped closer to the cleansing unit. A stream of light illuminated the inside when he flicked on that feature of his weapon.

"Shit!" Nala glanced at the damaged unit and couldn't see how Maze would have survived. She'd thought a stun grenade had been launched, that whining sound normally a warning of one, but there was massive

174

damage to the cleansing unit walls. They were bent inward, as if something had attached to them and blown.

"Who are you?" He kept his weapon and the beam of light on the cleansing unit.

"Captain Nala Vestria of the *Pride*."

"This is the *Varnish*." He pulled a second weapon, pointing it at her. "What in the hell is going on here? Why are you with cyborgs? That *is* a cyborg, isn't it?"

"My freighter was attacked." She decided to fudge the truth. The uniform he wore was the same one her father had sported for twenty years in the military.

They weren't pirates. They worked for Earth Government.

"I woke up and found myself locked inside this room. That's the first one I've seen. He showed up about a minute before you arrived. We didn't exactly speak. I huddled down here, terrified, and then you breached the door."

It worked. He lowered the weapon pointed at her, slid it into his holster, and focused solely on the cleansing unit. "It's a fucking cyborg. I thought the rumors were bullshit. Gray skin and all...but it looks like they bleed red."

She tried not to panic. Was Maze dead? Seriously injured? He wasn't making any sounds or attacking the soldier. She slowly got to her feet. Her back and ass hurt from the impact with the wall and floor, assuring her she'd have bruises. "Did you come to rescue me?"

The soldier turned his head. "No. We were posted inside this core to monitor the system. Imagine our surprise when we saw a shuttle fly in. We identified it as a well-known slaver."

Nala managed to keep her mouth from falling open. That couldn't be. She didn't believe Stag and his crew were into kidnapping people and selling them on the black market. "The *Varnish* is a slave-runner shuttle?"

He looked away from her and bent, running his light over the interior of the cleansing unit. "Yeah. It disappeared about ten years ago, according to the records we pulled up on it when the ID came in. Specifically, they stole women from colonies and sold them to brothels. It's why we didn't just blow it up and decided to board."

"I don't understand."

He scanned her from head to toe. "We've been stuck inside this shithole for three months. Our replacements don't come for another three. It gets lonely, you know? We weren't going to blow up women in need of our help."

"I see." She masked her features, trying to hide her disgust. She suspected they weren't on a rescue mission. They were looking for kidnapped women they could victimize further.

She must not have hidden her reaction well enough.

"Don't get all offended. We're saving you from doing dozens of men a day if these things had sold you to a brothel. There're only seven of us. We'll treat you right, and you'll get to go home once they send a shuttle to our monitoring station to change out the shifts. Do you know if any other women were taken?" He licked his lips. "We were hoping we wouldn't have to share."

"I have no idea."

"We'll find out. My unit will find them. Don't worry. We're going to treat you all *real* good."

"Thank you." They were tough words to get out. Nala seethed inside.

He looked away from her, back into the cleansing unit. "I should probably shoot it a couple more times just to make sure it never gets up again."

She took a few steps closer and worked up the nerve to peer inside the cleansing unit. The sight of Maze crumpled on the floor horrified her. He was in a ball, turned toward the wall, as if he'd tried to protect himself. His shirt was torn up, blood staining it. He'd managed to cover his face with his hands so she couldn't see if he'd taken damage there.

She did notice one of Maze's fingers twitch, and she gasped.

The soldier swung his head her way. "What?"

She reached out and gripped his arm. He'd kill Maze if he realized the cyborg was still alive. "It's just all sinking in. Thank you for saving me! I was terrified. I'm so grateful." She tried not to lay it on too thick but the guy *had* admitted he was there looking for women. She used her other hand and gripped the top of her shirt, pulling it down enough to flash some cleavage. "My heart feels as though it's going to pound right out of my chest. Can you see it?"

177

His gaze went right where she wanted, to the tops of her breasts. He was still bent over a bit and she threw her body forward, catching him off balance and unaware.

Thank God her father had taught her self-defense.

She thrust her elbow out, her fist against her chest where she still held her shirt, and slammed it into his ribs. They fell together and Nala landed on top of him, spreading her legs to quickly straddle the side of his thigh. She used her hold on his arm to keep it pinned down as she went for the sidearm he'd holstered. He hadn't fastened it, so it slid out easy. Nala fired before he could even recover.

He cried out, and the stench of burning material and flesh rose.

She hit the floor, rolled, and pointed the weapon at him again. The soldier writhed and jerked on his side. That's when Nala saw burn marks on the blue uniform—and the hole in his back.

She glanced at the weapon. It wasn't a stunner. She'd just blasted him with a laser that had cut right through him.

The man grabbed for his throat...but then stilled.

"Oh shit," she whispered. She managed to scoot closer, her hands shaking as she got to her knees then shoved his limp fingers away from his neck. She felt for a pulse above his uniform collar. There wasn't one.

The blast had gone out his back, probably through his lung on the way, and she figured it had done enough damage to stop his heart.

She'd killed an Earth Government soldier. He might have been a disgrace to military men, but it would still mean a death sentence for her.

A soft groan came from a few feet away and she turned her head. Maze attempted to sit up, and she swiftly tried to pull it together.

"I'm here. Maze? Can you hear me?" She crawled closer to the unit and paused at the edge of it.

He had turned his body, and was now sitting in the corner and cradling his injured arm. His eyes were open when he lifted his head, meeting her gaze. He looked as if he was disorientated and in a lot of pain.

"It's okay. Just stay down. You're really injured."

"I need my medical kit."

She didn't know where it was. There was the small one under the bunk in the wall drawer. "Okay. I'll get it."

A loud boom came from the corridor.

Nala twisted, landed on her ass again, and pointed the weapon in the direction of the still partially opened door. She braced her bare feet in front of her, spread her legs and sucked in huge gulps of air. Her hand still shook so she gripped the laser with both, locked her arms, and tried to judge where chest height would be, adjusting the tip of the weapon a little higher.

"Give me the weapon." Maze groaned and tried to scoot closer, judging from the sounds he made.

"I'll protect you." And she would.

Movement flashed, and she fired. Her aim was a little off and she hit one edge of the door, scarring the metal.

179

"Goddamn it," Stag shouted. "I thought you said you wouldn't try to kill me?"

She almost dropped the weapon. "I'm sorry! I didn't know it was you."

He hesitated then peered around the corner between the doors. It was hard to make him out in the dim red light, but she did. He stepped out from behind the wall of the corridor, gripped the sides of the door, and shoved. They groaned as he widened them before stepping inside.

"Put that down now," Stag demanded.

She dropped the weapon on the floor, the metal clattering. "Maze is hurt."

"I can see that." He hurried forward, kicked the weapon aside, and reached down.

She gasped when he gripped her upper arms and yanked her to her feet. He let go immediately. "Get out of the way."

Nala stumbled to the side as Stag crouched down next to the opening of the cleansing unit, checking on Maze. She remembered the medical kit and turned, hustling to retrieve it.

"Freeze!"

She did, mostly. Her head turned and she stared at a soldier who entered the room. He held a large weapon—and it was pointed at Stag. He glanced her way, and he couldn't hide his surprise. It only lasted for a heartbeat before he focused on Stag again.

"You move a fucking muscle and I'll blast a hole in you so big it will cut you in half."

She didn't move her head but she side-eyed Stag. He had his back to the soldier, still crouched at the opening of the cleansing unit. Nala focused on the soldier again.

He released the weapon with one hand, touched his ear, and spoke. "Come in. Someone answer me."

"Your team won't respond." Stag's voice came out calm and cold. "I take it you boarded after the first seven. They are all dead."

Nala clenched her jaw. She wanted to yell at Stag for being a dumb shit. The soldier had what looked like a small cannon weapon pointed at him and Stag was taunting the man.

"You'll die too unless you lower that weapon and surrender," Stag continued. "I'll let you live if you do what I say."

The soldier visibly paled but that passed quickly, his cheeks turning red. Nala figured that was rage. The guy dropped his hand from his earpiece and gripped the large weapon with both hands. She feared he'd fire.

"Thank God!" She kept her voice low, afraid to startle the guy and make him twitch his finger on the trigger. "You've come to rescue me! I was transporting diamonds the size of baseballs from the mines on Rigger Planet. There're four crates of them hidden on some moon they stopped at. Don't kill him! That cyborg is the only one who knows where they stashed them. They're worth millions of credits."

Nala took a hesitant step forward. The other soldier had been a dirtball who'd willing admitted to wanting to rescue women just to victimize them. She hoped this one had morals just as low. "Our transport was attacked and the entire crew killed except me. They're slavers; they were planning on selling me. My father was Manny Vestria. He served twenty years in the military. I know how little they pay you. We can split it fifty-fifty. Think of all those credits."

The soldier glanced at her. He didn't fire or adjust the weapon to aim at her, so she took a few more steps.

"We could be rich." She made it to the man's side, still holding his gaze. "They aren't very smart, and the cyborg won't move as long as you keep that weapon trained on him. Look."

He glanced at Stag.

It was the opening she was looking for.

She attacked, plowing into his arms and grabbed hold of his chest, fisting his uniform. She hooked one of his calves with the back of her heel, shoving as hard as she could with her other foot planted on the floor.

The man stumbled to the side and back, Nala stumbling with him. The weapon he still held fired, hitting something, but she knew she'd knocked into him hard enough that it wasn't Stag or Maze.

He flailed and Nala saw his fist coming at her. She winced in that split-second, but kept hold of his uniform and one leg, knowing it would be harder for him to fire the long weapon with her so close to his body and clinging to him.

182

Pain exploded in the side of her head and it dazed her. The sensation of falling registered before she hit the floor hard.

Someone yelled, a male, and that cannon blasted again.

Something hit her back, a sharp pain, but she couldn't move.

Then her body seemed to shut down from the agony inside her head, and she welcomed it.

Chapter Thirteen

Stag paced. "Why isn't she waking up?" He glared at Maze.

The medic wore a sling, his right arm out of commission until he healed. "She suffered a severe concussion."

"What about her back where that beam fell on top of her?" He worried it might have caused major damage. The soldier had managed to fire the weapon again when Stag had tackled him, hitting the ceiling with the blast. "It was heavy."

"I'm getting there."

"Hurry up! She could die because you're not treating her fast enough!"

"Stag." Hellion stepped between him and the medic. "He's doing his best. He had to stop the bleeding on his arm and stabilize the break in his wrist. It's left him one-handed. Nala is alive. Let him do his work without snapping at him every five seconds."

The lights came on and Stag clenched his teeth.

"Got it," Veller stated in his earpiece. "Life support is functioning. We didn't lose that."

"What did the soldiers do?" Stag resumed pacing.

"They blew a coupling to computer control, which shut it down, including power. I've managed to reroute around the damaged area. It will hold until we reach home but it's a mess. We're going to be grounded at least a week for repairs."

Stag wanted to hit something. "Kelis? Did you get those bodies off my shuttle?"

"Yes, Stag. Yammer and Parqel just returned. There's a group of pods attached to the rock wall about four thousand meters deeper inside. They used suits to float over and breach our hull. It's why another ship didn't register."

"What in the hell?" He was furious.

Yammer said, "Six pods, linked together. We accessed their computer. They were monitoring traffic in this solar system."

"How? The metals in this asteroid mess with sensors." Stag stopped pacing, watching Maze frown as he scanned Nala's stomach and pelvis area. He wanted to ask what was wrong but Yammer continued his report.

"They blasted two straight holes through the rock to the exterior and placed a direct link there to receive data uploads. There seems to be a small opening in the belt that allowed them to receive drone communications every three days, in fourteen-second intervals, before the signal is disrupted again. The drones are small, not easy to detect by any vessels. They stored all traffic information and forwarded it to the pods."

"Hold." Stag muted the coms. "What is wrong, Maze? Did you find something? You're scowling."

The medic glanced at him. "I don't have a full med bay here so I have to go over every inch of her carefully with a portable scanner. I haven't found any internal bleeding, nerve, or bone damage."

Stag spun around and turned on coms again. He couldn't stand to look at Nala lying on the bunk, looking so helpless. "Resume, Yammer. Did they have mission logs? Were they looking for us?"

"No. At least not officially."

"They believe they were tracking pirates, illegal traders, and possible Markus Model sightings," Parqel said next. "I accessed their personal journal logs. The one in charge assumed Earth Government might want to resume mining operations and they were sent to assess the threat to any miners sent here. Which means he wasn't too intelligent. They mined this section out years ago."

"Then why?" Stag just wanted answers.

"Unknown, but none of the personal journal logs mentioned anything about cyborgs." Parqel paused. "The last entry was made by their communications officer. They identified our shuttle as belonging to the criminal Earthers you took it from. They attacked us believing women were onboard, who they could steal. He seemed quite excited with the prospect of comforting any of them with sex. The entry was graphic. They fought and then voted over either blowing us up before we realized we weren't alone, or boarding us. It was a seven to one in favor of gaining women. The one you killed last was the holdout. It seems he refused to be a part of it, since they'd have gotten in trouble if anyone ever found out. They had planned to kill the women before a new shift arrived to relieve

186

them of duty. I guess he changed his mind and came after his crew to help them."

Stag clenched his teeth again. "Understood."

"I feel no guilt now for killing them," Hellion muttered. "They would have abused, murdered, and hidden the body of Nala if they'd taken us out. There's got to be a lot of crevices inside this tunnel to conceal a body."

"Or they could have incinerated a body," Maze snarled. "Earth Government military at its best. They called *us* murderers. At least we never took innocent lives."

"Stow it." Stag walked over to the panel and touched it. The computer responded, so he reached up and ripped off the annoying earpiece. He opened ship-wide coms. "We're online. Good work, Veller."

"Thank you. I'm heading to Control. Are you already there?"

Stag twisted around, staring at Nala. He should be at the helm, instead of waiting to see if she was going to recover. "I'm on my way too." He cut coms. "Maze? How is she?"

"I can go to Control if you want to stay." Hellion regarded him.

"It's my duty to be there, not yours."

"Are you certain of that? You're worried about her. You care. Stay with Nala. We can handle things without you for a while longer."

Stag debated it a second too long and Hellion exited the room before he could decide. He let it go, focusing on the medic instead. "Maze? You didn't answer me."

Maze straightened and peered at him with a grim look. "She saved both of our lives. You're aware of that, aren't you?"

"He would have hit *me* with his weapon, not you. What does that have to do with anything? I want an update on her medical condition."

"She'll be fine. I've found no life-threatening injuries."

Relief hit Stag, too much so. "Good. I should go to Control then. Stay with her, and once she's able to be moved, take her to your quarters. You can bunk with Hellion." He glanced at the damage to his room. "This one isn't livable until repairs are completed."

Maze moved into his path, blocking the door. "I shot the soldier found lying in the corridor. I was already injured when the second one planned to shoot me to make certain I never got up again. I was coming around, and I heard Nala flirting with him. I was convinced for a moment that she truly was happy to be rescued. That's when she attacked and killed that soldier. She protected me and saved my life."

"Your point?"

"She risked her life *twice* to save us both. You were wrong about her, Stag. Are you still planning on handing her over to the council when we reach Garden?"

"It's none of your business."

"It is now! She saved my life. I demand answers. Do you care about her? Have you changed your feelings about her enough to join a family unit with her?"

The question astonished him. He couldn't even speak.

"She chose cyborgs over Earth Government soldiers. Are you willing to keep her or not?"

Stag had enough. He stepped forward, his chest pressing against Maze's, and glared at him. "Get out of my way."

Maze didn't budge. He just glared back. "Are you going to do right by Nala? If not, I plan to join a family unit with her. Give her to me if you aren't willing to keep her."

Rage filled Stag. "She's my prisoner."

"That would imply she's the enemy. She chose sides, Stag. You're just being too stubborn to admit it."

"Perhaps she knew it would be a losing battle for them to go against us. Nala is smart."

"And perhaps you've grown so bitter over the years that you're unable to see the truth. Hand Nala over to the council and I'll petition to be her male. I owe her a life debt. That will take precedent over all others who apply." Maze walked over to the bed and picked up an injector.

"What are you giving her?"

"Why do you care?" Maze pressed it against her shoulder.

Stag crossed the room. "*What did you give her?*"

"Something for pain and healing, of course."

They glared at each other. Maze spoke first.

"I know you, Stag. I saw your reaction when she was down, and you believed her critically injured. Don't make the mistake of letting her go. Another male will work hard to secure her affections and loyalty. They will

189

offer her all the things you haven't so far. Females like her want a male who is kind and loving. You'll lose her forever. There's no shame in having a weakness when it brings you happiness. She's your one shot at it."

Stag glanced at Nala, not willing to get into an argument with the medic.

"You've been avoiding her, which means she poses a threat. But the only thing you fear is caring too much and opening yourself up to experiencing emotional pain. We escaped Earth to *live*, not just exist. Your motivation to face each morning shouldn't just be the next mission the council sends us on."

Stag sighed. "I'll think about what you've said. I need to go to Control. Move her when she can be."

Maze motioned to his arm in the sling. "How do you suppose I do that? Make her walk? No. I want her to stay immobile for at least six hours. She suffered some bruising to her back and minor swelling. It could be uncomfortable for her. I also protest giving up my quarters unless you're giving her to me. There's a better place on the *Varnish* to move her."

Stag held his gaze.

"It has always been courteous of you to put yourself in quarters equal to those of your crew—but that was before you had a female. She would be more comfortable in the captain's quarters."

"That space is for when one of the council wants to travel with us, or when we take on extra crew members so they aren't forced to sleep inside a cargo hold."

Maze shook his head. "We haven't had to use it in over a year, Stag. I cleaned and stocked it after you brought Nala onboard, hoping you'd take her there. The spare bunks have been removed. She'll be more comfortable recovering there than in my quarters. Do it for her."

Stag knew it was the best option.

"Parqel, Veller, and Kelis will refuse to share their quarters with anyone. They tend to pick arguments. Yammer makes everyone uncomfortable by staring as though he's plotting our deaths. He hates his personal space invaded. That leaves Hellion. Don't make me bunk with him. Please. He'll drive me insane while I'm healing. I just want to sleep but he'll attempt endless conversations. I'll be sure to tell the crew I talked you into it, and they'll be grateful."

Stag finally grinned ruefully. "All of that is true. I'll take her to the captain's quarters. Can she be moved now?"

"Yes."

"Get out of the way then and walk ahead of us. You're going to have to activate the lift and the door."

"Of course."

Stag stepped closer to his bunk, afraid he'd hurt her. He bent, very carefully sliding his arms under Nala, and lifted. He adjusted her so her head rested on his chest. Her stillness left him uneasy.

"She's drugged." Maze seemed to read his anxiety. "I wanted her to stay asleep until she healed more."

Stag turned. "Let's go."

They left his quarters and made it to the lift. Maze activated it and Stag stepped inside, hugging a wall to make room for the medic. They went up to Control level and met Yammer when the doors opened.

"You're taking her to captain's quarters?" He moved back.

Stag stiffened, expecting the male to protest. "Yes."

"Good. I'm not sharing *my* room, and Hellion is bitching about how he told everyone this was a shit mission and he seems convinced we're doomed until we reach home." Yammer smiled at Maze. "Good job. I know this is your doing. But you were motivated, since I also know you would have been the poor bastard stuck with him. Need help removing the wall bunks and storing them? I'm on my way back to cargo two anyway."

"I already did that, but thank you." Maze got out of the lift first.

Stag followed, carrying Nala, but paused to address Yammer. "How bad is the damage down there?"

"Nothing we want to fix until we're doing ground repairs. They hacked the access pad and made a mess of it to open the docking door. The outer panel is sealed though, so we're good. It's not as if we're planning on opening it again until we have to offload those bots."

"Did they mess with the crates?"

"They're marked mining equipment." Yammer shook his head. "They had no interest in that." He peered down at Nala. "How bad is she?"

"She'll be fine." Maze cleared his throat. "After she gets plenty of rest in a bed. That would be *this* way…"

192

Stag rolled his eyes and stepped around Yammer. "Keep me updated on repairs."

"Will do."

Maze opened the doors to the captain's quarters and turned on the lights.

Stag felt surprised when he looked around, noting all the differences since he'd last been in there. "You've been busy."

Maze turned. "I put down the larger bed from the wall cabinet and placed shelves where the bunks were attached, to hide the connecters. I wanted it to feel homier for Nala. I even downloaded books and entertainment vids for her enjoyment. Don't worry. I knew you'd be wary of her having access to the computer, so it's contained. She can adjust the lights, watch vids, and use the pad next to the bed to read preloaded novels. I locked down the shields over the viewing ports but I'd suggest you allow her access to them. It will help her feel less contained if she can see space."

His medic's attention to detail irritated the hell out of Stag.

Maze walked over to the large bed and pulled back the covers and blankets. "You should undress her and put her under the covers. She'll be more comfortable. I can do it if you're not comfortable with her nudity."

"You've gone to a lot of time and trouble thinking about Nala's needs when she doesn't belong to you."

"Someone had to."

Stag crossed the room and gently put Nala down on the bed. He straightened, the urge to punch Maze filling him.

Maze was obviously aware of his anger and backed away. "Calm down. There's a lot on this ship that I'm not permitted to do. You don't trust me to take a shift at the helm, nor do shuttle repairs. I have a lot of spare time on my hands, and that means thinking of the wellbeing of everyone aboard the *Varnish*, including Nala. It wasn't meant as an insult to your ability to care for her."

That deflated his temper. "Thank you."

"The crew will accept you keeping her, if that's a concern of yours."

Stag had neglected his duties for long enough. "I don't have time to discuss this anymore. Stay with her. I need to go to Control."

"She was a freighter captain, Stag. I've tried to think of all the excuses you'd come up with to avoid keeping her. She left her own planet to live in space. I highly doubt she'd prefer Garden over this ship, if given the choice. Some of the crew will most likely not be pleased, but you could reassign them elsewhere if they don't adjust. The *Varnish* is your personal property. I know Hellion and I will have no problem with Nala as crew."

"Maze, I really need to get to Control. It's possible that the pirates might check the asteroid belt for us."

"Veller is more than qualified to kill if the need arises. Your place right now is with Nala. She's *your* female, she saved *your* life, and I'm betting it's *your* face she'll appreciate seeing when she wakes." Maze turned. "You stay and care for her. I'll go from section to section and send you reports. Get her comfortable, and you might want to wash some of that blood off her." The door closed behind him.

Stag just stood there, unsure what to do.

He finally turned, his gaze on Nala. He could have lost her.

He had a lot of thinking to do. But first, he'd do exactly what Maze had suggested. He walked into the expanded cleansing unit and got warm, wet cloths, and returned to the bed, taking a seat.

He washed the blood off her as gently as he could and stripped off her clothing, seeing the bruising on her lower back firsthand. The one higher on her back, the one he'd put there with his knee while he'd been injured, had almost faded away.

"What am I going to do with you, Nala?" He wished the answer was simple.

Chapter Fourteen

Nala opened her eyes and stared at an unfamiliar ceiling. Memory came back instantly, and she tensed. Stag's ship had been boarded by the military.

Motion to her right had her jerking her head, staring into a pair of very familiar blue eyes in a handsome face.

Stag smiled. "I'm here, Nala."

"The soldiers?" She wanted to sit up but he leaned over her, keeping her from rising.

"Disposed of."

She let her body relax, understanding that the boarding party was no longer a threat. "How is your crew?"

"They are fine. Maze had the worst of the injuries but he'll recover fast. A broken wrist, and the cuts along his arm were superficial."

"What about you?" She glanced down, taking in as much of his body as she could, not seeing any tears in his uniform or signs of injury.

"I'm fine. They never stood a chance against my crew of cyborgs. The military caught us by surprise but it wasn't enough of an advantage." He took a deep breath. "Maze was the only one hurt, besides you." He reached up and caressed her cheek. "How do you feel?"

"A little weird."

"Maze gave you a shot to dull the pain."

She shifted her attention to the ceiling, around the parts of the room she could see, then back to him. "Where are we?"

"The captain's quarters."

"Your ship was destroyed and you took me over to the soldiers' ship?"

"No. We're still onboard mine."

She evaluated that in her head. "I'm confused. You're the captain, right? So whose quarters were we in before?"

"Mine. I never stay in here."

"Why not? It's much more spacious." She peered at the bed then met his gaze again. "Larger sleeping space too."

"I felt it gave me equal footing with my crew."

"By taking crew quarters instead of this one?"

"Yes."

"Having the most comfortable living space on a ship is one of the perks of being the one signing their checks."

"We don't use a monetary system."

"I still don't understand. Why do your men work for you then?"

He smiled. "Cyborgs get free food, clothing, and living accommodations. We never ask for more than we need. Everyone in my society finds a job that they enjoy, and we provide for each other. My crew chooses to serve on the *Varnish*. We only use your credit system when we trade with Earthers. Credits are useless to us otherwise. Is there anything else you'd like to know?"

She swallowed. "Why are you being so nice and friendly to me?"

His expression appeared almost tender, and the way he looked at her...as if she were precious... "Why wouldn't I? Are you thirsty? Hungry? Tell me what you need and I'll get it for you."

Fear hit hard. "Crap. I'm dying, aren't I?"

He scowled. "No. Why would you say that?"

"Because you're being so...unlike you. You're answering my questions, you just told me the actual name of your ship, and you smiled without me having to try really hard to make it possible." She reached up and pushed at his chest. "Move. Are my legs gone or something? Was I shot after that jerk punched me? Do I have internal bleeding Maze can't repair since nobody probably has my blood type on this ship?"

He straightened. "You're fine, Nala. A little bruised, and you sustained a mild concussion. Maze assured me you'll fully recover."

She sat up, shoved the bedding to her thighs, and stared at her naked body. That came as a surprise.

"I undressed you and cleaned off some blood. There was a fair bit. I attacked the soldier you distracted and his blood sprayed over you when I killed him."

She ran her hands over her body, even kicked off the covers from her legs and made sure everything was there. "Ten fingers and toes."

"Stop. You're acting irrational, and it's making me concerned about your mental state."

She met his gaze. "How long have I been out? Did we reach your home planet? Is this the big kiss off, where you finally get to tell me good riddance and hand me over to some other cyborg?"

"No. We're still tethered inside the mining core to avoid pirates locating us. I estimate we won't reach Garden for another few days. And why would you say that?"

"Because you're being so damn nice and...well, you said it. *Concerned.* That's not you, Stag. Just give it to me straight. What horrible thing do you have to tell me that would make you pity me enough to act this way?"

His mouth twisted downward more.

"Just spit it out! I can take it. It's got to be super bad."

He inhaled and slowly blew it a breath. "I've decided not to let you go."

"You already told me that. I didn't know it was up for debate. You said you wouldn't trust me not to tell the authorities that cyborgs are alive and actually roaming space. You're also paranoid and don't trust me one tiny bit."

"*I* am keeping you, Nala. I'm not handing you over to Cyborg Council to assign you to another male. You're *mine*."

She could say a lot about Stag, usually, but at that moment, he'd left her speechless. She just gaped at him, astounded.

He reached up and ran his fingers through his hair. "I'm screwing this up. I'm not good at expressing myself." He dropped his hand on the bed and sighed. "You saved my life."

That made more sense. "So you feel grateful to me, or indebted, and you think keeping me with you is nicer than handing me over to some stranger?"

"I have decided to keep you. I am relieved that you chose me over your chance of escape."

Her heart beat faster. "What do you mean by that? Clarify the keeping me part."

His eyes narrowed and he leaned in closer. His mouth parted—but then the door chimed. Stag moved fast, gripping the bedding and jerking it up, covering her. A few seconds later, Maze entered.

"I came to check on my patient."

"Never enter my quarters without permission." Stag rose to his feet and faced off against Maze.

"I apologize." Maze smiled at Nala. "How are you feeling? Is the pain manageable? Do you have a headache? Dizziness? Nausea?"

"Am I dying or something? Tell it to me straight, Maze. You're a medic, so you had to take some kind of oath to be honest to a patient. I'm demanding that now."

His smile faded. "You're going to be fine. Why would you think otherwise?"

She hugged the bedding to her chest with one arm to keep it from slipping down and exposing her breasts and jerked her thumb toward Stag. "Did he get punched in the head too? Something is wrong with him."

Maze glared at Stag. "I told you to be kind and loving to her, so she'll agree to stay with you. How could you mess that up?" Maze held her gaze next, his features softening. "Stag was frightened when you were hurt, and realized he didn't want to lose you. He has feelings where you are concerned. He doesn't want to allow another male to have you, Nala. You matter to him. He's horrible at expressing his emotions, this is new to him, but he—"

Clarity slammed into Nala hard, and she interrupted. "Shut up, Maze. That's enough. Thanks. Now go away."

He blinked, his lips still parted.

"Go." She waved her hand. "Shoo. Bye. Stag and I need to be alone."

The medic spun and stormed out the door, muttering something under his breath as he went.

"Don't enter my quarters again without permission," Stag yelled after him.

The door sealed and Nala watched Stag. He finally looked back at her. His blue eyes were hooded, a frown marring his features. Seconds ticked by, utterly silent ones, as she tried to wrap her head around what she'd learned.

"First off, you scared the crap out of me. You, suddenly being nice out of the blue, are frightening. Second, why would you listen to anything Maze told you to do? Do you know who you *aren't* like? *Him*. Is any of what he just said true?"

Stag hesitated but then nodded.

Nala grinned.

"It's not amusing."

"It kind of is." She patted the bed next to her. "Come here."

He didn't budge.

"Please?"

Stag reluctantly moved, taking a seat.

"Thank you. I feel for you too, if that helps. Just be yourself from now on though. The man I've gotten to know would just tell me he's keeping me."

"I stated that."

"Are you still going to tie me to the bed every night, worried I might choke you?"

"No."

"Lock me in the room?"

"Are you going to try to escape?"

"Are you going to make me want to get away from you?"

"We're negotiating terms now?" That appeared to make him angry.

"Let's just say if you teach me more about cyborg society—specifically, how you might impress a woman enough to stay with you—I'd be less likely to want to escape."

"You expect me to take orders from you?" His tone sharpened, turning gruff. "You want to control my life?"

"No. That's not who you are. I meant the sex parts. You could school me a lot and keep me too tired to want to get out of your bed. I really enjoyed when you taught me about oral sex and stamina."

A mischievous glint showed in his eyes. "That might imply I want you to join a family unit with me."

"I don't fully understand what that entails, but I'm willing if it means we stay together long-term. I won't agree to stay if you keep threatening to hand me over to your council."

"You don't have a say in the matter. I'm keeping you, Nala. You belong to me. Every time I sleep, you'll be in my bed with me. I won't ever let you go."

"You have to stop tying me to the bed. That's a sticking point with me."

"Sometimes I might do it if you misbehave, and I want to...school you properly. You tend to wiggle around a lot when I'm between your thighs."

"Fair enough. Plus, really hot. Do I ever get to tie *you* up? You seemed to enjoy it that one time."

"We'll negotiate that later."

"You mean when you've outgrown your paranoia and are certain I won't suffocate you with your own pillow?"

He cracked a smile. "Yes."

"I can work with that."

He inched closer. "I couldn't stand the thought of losing you. I won't."

"Good. I've grown attached to you too. I told you, you die, I cry. I meant that."

"You can't compartmentalize your body from your feelings."

"No."

"I'll have to use that to my advantage."

She smiled. "I totally believe you will." She cupped his face and kissed him.

He groaned deeply, wrapping his arm around her and pulling her tight against him.

She gasped, feeling pain, and broke the kiss.

Stag cursed, jerking his arm away from her. "I forgot about your back. You're injured and need a few days to recover."

"I could be on top. I want you, Stag."

A chime sounded, and they both cursed.

"Your crew has shit timing."

"Tell me about it." He pulled away from her, rose up, and crossed the room. He slapped his hand on the pad next to the door. "What?"

Nala watched him. He didn't speak again, but his expressions changed, as if he were reacting to a silent conversation. He didn't look pleased when he dropped his hand and sighed, staring at her.

"I need to go to Control. I won't be long. I'll get food if you're hungry."

"I'm good, but could you arrange it so I can contact you if I need to?"

He nodded and placed his hand back on the pad, keeping eye contact with her the entire time. "Done. Just say my name. I put it on audio command so you don't have to get out of bed. The speaker coms will be active."

"Thanks."

"Rest. Get better." He reached down, adjusting the front of his pants. "*Sooner* would be better."

She grinned. "I like that I make you hard."

He left without commenting.

Nala lay back and felt happy. Her cyborg wanted to keep her. The L word hadn't been exchanged but they had built the foundation for that. His wanting her said it all. "Stag?"

"What's wrong, Nala?"

"Nothing. I was just making sure it worked. I think my back will be fine if I stay off it and on top of you. I did love that position."

"I remember. You're going to make me enter Control with an erection. I knew you were trouble."

"I guess your crew will figure out we're doing more than just sleeping in your bed."

"I'll make certain that they do. I know some of them have made you offers. They won't do that again."

"Good. And Stag? I'm the fun kind of trouble. I'll show you when you get back."

"I need to address this situation. Behave. Stag out."

"Okay." Coms silenced, and she chuckled.

Stag stormed into Control, glaring at Maze. His entire crew had assembled there, and he had a feeling it was the medic's fault. "What's going on? What is the emergency?"

"Maze stated you're keeping the female." Veller stepped forward, glowering. "I protest."

"It's not your call, Veller," Yammer replied, crossing his arms.

"I think it's wonderful." Hellion grinned. "I like Nala."

"You like everyone," Kelis rasped. "What do *you* think, Parqel? I'm neutral. Stag did tell us we could keep one of the sex bots."

Parqel shrugged. "The *Varnish* belongs to Stag. He can keep the Earther if he wants. As I said before he arrived, it's none of our business."

"Exactly." Maze pointed at Veller. "You're the only one with a problem with it. You can transfer duties once we reach Garden and assign yourself to another vessel."

"I like *this* one because there are no females aboard. And put your hand down."

Maze lowered his arm. "You're outvoted."

"Well, now it *has* a female aboard, and I'm glad," Hellion said. "It means we can get females too one day."

"You only say that because no one else wants to work with you, so you're stuck on the *Varnish*."

"That's right, Veller." Hellion's good humor faded and he advanced, his hands tightening into fists. "This is my home, more so than yours. Nala stays. You go."

Stag was done. He'd feared keeping Nala might have an adverse effect on his crew, and he'd been right. A few of them appeared ready to fight. "Enough!"

All the men looked at him at the loud bellow.

"It's not a vote or up for debate. Nala belongs to me. You are more than welcome to no longer assign yourself to *my* ship once we reach Garden, Veller."

The male grimly regarded him. "You're really set on allowing an Earther to live on your ship?"

It was an easy answer for Stag. "Yes. She stays."

Veller snarled and spun, pacing the floor.

"I don't know what your problem is, nor do I care." Stag watched him warily, prepared if he attacked. "And this was a brilliant idea, Maze."

"I figured you might delay informing them of your decision. I had hoped they would all agree Nala might be a good thing for this entire crew."

"Anyone touches her and I remove their fingers." Stag gripped his sidearm. "I'm not sharing her. I'll allow you to keep two sex bots. You can figure out where to store them though. I don't want them leaving the crew quarters area."

"That's agreeable to me." Parqel smiled.

"I didn't mean Nala should sleep with us." Maze shook his head. "You micromanage us all, Stag. Nala will keep you occupied and give the rest of us more responsibilities. You can be a bit overbearing."

Veller paused, interest finally showing on his features. "That's true. I didn't think of that."

Hellion snorted. "You can take the helm more often. That makes you happy, doesn't it? Stag won't work as many shifts if he has a female."

"Can I lead a mission?" Veller stepped closer. "Just one? You'll need to bond with that female. That means you should spend a good week or two with her. Perhaps you could do it on Garden. You can trust me with the *Varnish*."

"Earthers have honeymoons. I remember that. It's where they enclose themselves and have lots of sex." Kelis nodded. "We could go on a mission without you, Stag."

"Over my dead body are you getting me to leave my own ship." Stag considered Veller's request briefly. "I will let you lead a mission, though but I'm staying onboard. I don't like spending time on Garden. It's why I went to the trouble of stealing this shuttle."

"So we have a plan." Hellion grinned widely. "Nala stays. Everyone is happy. Stag spends more time with the Earther so he's not too controlling with us."

"And we get two sex bots instead of one." Yammer smiled too. "I like this compromise."

Stag eased his hold off his weapon. "Are we done here? I'd like to return to the captain's quarters. I'll be staying there from now on. Nala and I need the extra room."

"There's our answer to the sex bots. We can store them in your old quarters when they aren't in use." Parqel nodded. "Once we do repairs, of course."

"Veller, you're in charge." Stag spun, leaving Control.

It could have gone a lot worse. It would be difficult hiding two sex bots aboard his ship, keeping them from the council, but his crew deserved something for all the dangerous missions they went on. It wouldn't be the first time he'd left something out of his reports.

He smiled, entering his new quarters. Nala waited—and it felt good.

Chapter Fifteen

Ten days later

Stag sat at the helm, checking systems.

"Everything is perfect," Hellion stated from a few feet away. "We went over every inch of the *Varnish* while we were grounded on Garden doing repairs. Go spend time with your Nala. We have this."

"We do," Veller agreed. "As you can see, we're on course to Gerard Station. We'll be there in approximately eleven hours."

Stag turned his head, staring at Kelis sitting at weapons control. "Do you have anything to add?"

"It's a simple mission, one we can easily handle. Two of us will dress up to hide what we are and interview the survivor of the pod that landed there."

"We have the authority uniforms in our hold." Hellion smiled. "We will be on and off that station within an hour, two max."

The doors to Control opened and Nala entered. She walked straight to Stag and sat down across his lap, wrapping her arms around his neck. "Are you driving your crew nuts again? You were supposed to be getting us food but I knew I'd find you here instead."

"Don't make me regret giving you free access to the shuttle." He kept his tone soft though, playful. He found it amusing that she'd hunted him down.

"What are we talking about?" She glanced away from him to his crew.

"Someone reported being attacked by a cyborg." Hellion answered first. "We're going to interview the survivor. It will be another false lead, but we always check them out."

"Can't you just ask other cyborg ships if they did it?" She peered at Stag.

"We are always hopeful other cyborgs escaped Earth. We weren't able to free all of them when we left. Sometimes reports of sightings are made, and we always hope to find survivors to take them home to Garden."

"The last time someone said they'd captured a cyborg, it was an Earther mechanic who fell into engine fluid and his skin had been turned blue." Hellion chuckled. "The authorities held him for two days before figuring it out."

Kelis laughed.

"That's horrible. Poor guy." Nala made a face, scrunching her nose.

"It was funny," Stag admitted. "This time, a supply shuttle was attacked and one survivor made it into a pod that reached the Gerard station. We're on our way there now."

Nala tensed and climbed off his lap. "Display that sector on the main screen, please."

No one moved.

"Come on." Nala glared at Stag. "I said *please*. I know this route well. I used to deliver to that station. It's a big entertainment one."

"Do it," Stag ordered.

Nala turned, strode to the front of Control, and waited. The map showed up. "Amplify this section here, please?" She used her finger to motion where she wanted.

Stag nodded at Hellion.

Nala pointed. "This is Gerard Station." She pointed to a blip close to it. "This is Erosa. It's a breathable planet with a few thousand residents. They grow food." She pointed to another blimp. "This is the Arris Station. It's bad news. It's crime central, and I avoided docking there." She turned briefly, facing his crew. "Now here's the interesting part."

She faced the screen again, pointing to three grouped moons. "Captains talk frequently. A lot of freighters were hired to take dome habitats to this center moon right here." She put her finger on it, then looked over her shoulder, holding Stag's gaze. "They were hired by the military. EG is setting up operations on this moon. Based on what they ordered, I'd guess a few hundred soldiers will be stationed there. I don't know if it's operational, but it's a only few hours' fly time from Gerard Station. Rumor is the colony on Erosa asked them to come because of the traffic going to Arris. They worried about being robbed since, as I said, it's crime central. Arris Station visitors have left the Gerard Station and the planet alone so far but..." She shrugged. "That could change. Be careful."

"Shit," Hellion muttered. "That's bad."

Nala continued to study the monitor. "I'd fly by way of the Quellis sector and bypass those moons entirely. That way, if they *are* operational and get an alert, we could be in and out of there before they have a chance to send soldiers to the station. That is, if you still want to interview the one who claimed to see a cyborg."

Stag stood. "What would you do, Veller?"

The male didn't appear thrilled with what he'd learned. He seemed to think about it. "Do you think your information is accurate, Nala?"

"Yes."

"I'd change course. Stag trusts you, and that's good enough for me. It will add a day to our travel but we can avoid entering the moon's sensor range for as long as possible."

Stag crossed the room to Nala and surprised her by scooping her into his arms. "We'll be in our quarters. It's your mission. Only contact me if it's an emergency."

Nala wrapped her arms around his neck and rested her cheek against her chest. He carried her back to their quarters and sealed the door.

"Did you hear that? Veller trusts me."

He chuckled. "He said *I* trust you."

"Close enough."

He took a seat on the bed, adjusting her on his lap. "Thank you for sharing that intel with us."

"Your crew is my crew. I'm only looking out for them."

His eyes narrowed.

She laughed. "We'll work on that one still. Sharing is caring. It's a good motto." She kissed his chin, then nibbled on his lower lip, finally pulling back. "What about food? I specifically remember you promised me a meal."

He twisted, tossing her on the bed and pinning her under him. "I *specifically* remember ordering *you* to stay inside our quarters. I think you need to be taught a lesson."

Her blue eyes sparkled. "The hot, sexy kind?"

"You're not supposed to look so excited when I threaten you."

"You don't scare me anymore." She slid her fingers into his hair, playing with it. "You're a big softy."

He adjusted his body, wiggling his hips between her thighs. She spread them for him and he pressed his groin against hers. "What were you saying about soft?"

She suddenly sobered and he wondered what he'd said wrong.

"I love you, Stag."

Her admission didn't surprise him. He'd suspected she had strong feelings for him. But he was surprised by his reaction. Joy hit—a powerful emotion that tightened his chest.

"I know you love me too. You just don't say it because you're a badass cyborg and it's going to take time to wear you down until you become more wordy. Your actions tell me what your mouth can't."

He smiled. "Is that so?"

"Yes."

He slid down her, gripped the front of her pants, and began to remove them. "Let's put that to a test. I think I'm very skilled with using my mouth to express my feelings."

She grinned. "Give me your worst, cyborg."

He paused, holding her gaze. "You've become the heart of me, Nala. I'll only ever give you my best."

Made in the USA
Lexington, KY
27 September 2016